# PERSIAN WARRIORS

MITRA KIAEE

Serial Number: P2345250127

Title: Persian Warriors

Sub Tittle: The stories of the heroes are adapted from the  epic poetry collection called " Shahnameh" by Ferdowsi

Writer: Mitra Kiaee

ISBN: 978-1-990760-97-6

Metadata: Epic / Heroic

Illustrator: Nashmin Valadi

Cover Design: Mahboobeh Laalpoor

Book: Paperback

Pages: 182

Publish Date: October 2023

Publisher: Kidsocado Publishing House

Kidsocado Publishing House

Vancouver, Canada

Phone : +1 (833) 633 8654

WhatsApp: +1 (236) 333 7248

Email: info@kidsocado.com

https://kidsocadopublishinghouse.com

https://kphclub.com

# Preface

Hakim Abolghasem Ferdowsi was born in 329 AH in Tabran, Tous, to a wealthy father. He acquired knowledge and wisdom, was fascinated by stories, and treasured Iran's history. In the fourth century, Daqiqi, a young Zoroastrian poet, started to compose Iran's national stories. By order of the Samanid king, Daqiqi was tasked with turning the Shahnameh of Abu-Mansur from prose to poetry. He had only versified a thousand couplets when he was killed at a young age (approx. 367 to 369 AH), and a vast majority of the stories of Shahnameh were left unfinished. Ferdowsi continued his unfinished task, and started to write the Shahnameh in 370 or 371. At first, Ferdowsi was incredibly wealthy, and some of Khorasan's elders, who were interested in ancient Iranian history, lent him a helping hand. Over time, after Ferdowsi had versified most of Shahnameh, he became impecunious Ferdowsi only started to compose the Shahnameh for his own interest years before Sultan Mahmud had come to power. However, since he lost his wealth and youth to this end, he contemplated presenting it to a great king. Assuming that Sultan Mahmud would see its worth, he journeyed to Ghazni. It is not known why the sultan did not find gratification in the Shahnameh. Some say that by the slander of the envious, Ferdowsi was accused of atheism before Ferdowsi only started to compose the Shahnameh for his own interest years before Sultan Mahmud had come to power. However, since he lost his wealth and youth to this end, he contemplated presenting it to a great king. Assuming that Sultan Mahmud would see its worth, he journeyed to Ghazni. It is not known why the sultan did not find gratification in the Shahnameh. Some say that by the slander of the envious, Ferdowsi was accused of atheism before Mahmud, and some of the court's poets were malcontent of Ferdowsi; Therefore, they spoke ill Shanameh's stories to Iran's old heroes. Hence, Sultan Mahmud considered the Shahnameh lacking in substance, cast aspersions upon Rostam, and raged against Ferdowsi. "The Shahnameh is nothing but the tale of Rostam," he declared, "and there are thousands of Rostams in my army."

It is said that Ferdowsi was furious about Sultan's defiance, disparaged him in several couplets, and then, fearing persecution, left Ghazni. For some time, he was a fugitive in Herat, Rey, and Tabarestan, went from city to city, and finally found eternal peace in his birthplace, Tous. Some have dated his death to 411, and others 416 AH. Ferdowsi was buried in Tous in an orchard belonging to himself.

Years later, Mahmud occasionally recollected Ferdowsi and regretted his debasement of him. He decided to atone for the past, and sent much treasure to him. However, the poet's body was departing on the day Sultan's gift was on its way to Tous. Ferdowsi left a daughter for posterity, for his son had died in his living days; it is said that Ferdowsi's daughter rejected and returned Sultan Mahmud's gift.

# Keyumars

The first king of the world was Keyumars. In those days, humans lived in caves and wore animal hides. He started breeding animals for the people for their milk and meat. Keyumars had a handsome and skilled son named Siamak. They lived happily for a long time and had no foe but Ahriman. Ahriman had a vicious and warring son who was vexed by the enthronement of Siamak. He, therefore, assembled a massive army and invaded Keyumars' dominion. Soroush came to Siamak wearing a tiger's hide and delivered the news.

The young prince went to battle Ahriman with his army, and was slain by the demon. Keyumars was informed of Siamak's death and wept and mourned for him for a year. At last, Soroush suggested to gather an army to fight the wicked demon. The king faced the sky, uttered Yazata's name, and hastened to battle Ahriman. Siamak had an intelligent and cultured son named Hushang. Before the battle, Keyumars revealed all secrets to him, making him the master of animals and humans. The two armies faced off, and the war commenced. Keyumars stopped Ahriman at every turn, took him in his claws, and killed him; after thirty years of rule, he departed this world.

# Hushang

Hushang succeeded his grandfather on the throne at the age of forty. He made the world prosperous and just, and managed to extract iron from ore. One day, he climbed the mountain with several companions. Suddenly, he saw a tall black creature. He grasped a rock and hurled it at it with all the strength his arm could muster. The small rock smashed against a bigger one, the spark ignited a fire, and Hushang thanked the Lord for the discovery. At night, they made fire, and sat around and celebrated with his nation. This is known as the Sadeh festival (10th of Bahman), left from him as a remembrance.

With fire and iron, he spread blacksmithing and built the tools for agriculture and hunting, then decided to create the means for easier sea travel. With the help of blacksmiths, he started to build new things, and taught people to plant seeds and farm. He separated cows, donkeys, and sheep from the rest of the animals, and tended for them. Then, he chose the animals with warm wool, and made clothes for his people. Eventually, he left this world, leaving behind only his noble name.

## Tahmuras

After Hushang, his son Tahmuras took the throne. He swore to put an end to evil and free people from the yoke of demons. At his time, they spun goat and sheep wool into yarn to knit clothes. He trained goshawks and falcons to hunt for the people. He also used hens and roosters, among other domesticated animals. He had an adviser named Shahrasb, who was devout and always guided the king toward good deeds. A ray of divine light had illuminated the king's essence, and he went to fight the devils, captured many, and killed the rest. The captives begged to be left alive and offered to teach them literacy. Tahmuras accepted, and humans learned to read and write. Over thirty years, he created wisdom and arts, and then died.

# Jamshid

After Tahmuras, Jamshid was enthroned. All creatures, including humans, demons, and animals, obeyed him. Over fifty years, he built iron weapons. Textiles were made with silk, cotton, and fur during his reign. He founded various communities, and fostered craft among the people. He sent the clerics up a mountain to pray to God alone. He trained a group named Neysarian, and turned them into brave warriors. The farmers, too, started to cultivate and work.

By Jamshid's order, the demons mixed water and earth to make mud, and started to build geometrically-shaped buildings, and the people were given homes and bathhouses. He managed to extract rubies, pearls, gold, and silver. He discovered the scent of perfume, and spearheaded the advancement of medicine and treatments. He built ships to traverse the seas. Jamshid's fifty-year rule brought progress and prosperity. He then built himself a magnificent throne. One day, he climbed on top, and the demons lifted him. People gathered around him and rejoiced. They named that day Newroz (Persian New Year), which lives on to this day. Three-hundred years passed, and there were no deaths. Then, Jamshid became arrogant and disobeyed the Lord. He called the elders, and said, "You owe your comfort to me, and I have created art, wisdom, and medicine; Therefore, I am god."

# Zahhak

A faithful and fair Arab man named Moradas used to live during the reign of Jamshid. He had a wicked and devilish son named Zahhak. Satan would see him daily to give him advice, and Zahhak would heed his words. One day, Satan asked him to kill his father and take his place. Zahhak was vexed, for he did not want to be his father's murderer. Satan promised that if he did, he would make him ascendant.

When Moradas woke up early in the morning to pray, Zahhak threw him into a well in the orchard, killed him, and took his father's place. Satan came to him as a fairy, and went into the kitchen. He was a skilled chef, and made delicious foods. Zahhak thanked him, and asked him to give him what he had promised. Satan took the opportunity and asked permission to kiss his shoulders, and Zahhak allowed him. Satan did so and disappeared. Instantly, two black serpents sprouted out of Zahhak's shoulders. He looked for a cure and tried cutting them off, but they grew back. Many physicians gathered around him to find a cure, but they failed. Satan came to him as a doctor, saying, "You need to calm them by feeding them human brains so that they leave you alone." With this trick, the devil wanted to rid the world of humanity.

Jamshid's army turned their backs on him; for he had become a tyrannical infidel. They left him and went to Zahhak in the land of Arabs. Zahhak assembled a massive army and set his sights on Iran. Luck had turned against Jamshid, so he fled and left the Kayanian crown and throne to Zahhak. After one-hundred years, they found him in the Sea of China, and Zahhak sliced Jamshid in half with his saw. At that time, Jamshid was seven-hundred. Years passed and thousands joined Zahhak. All good deeds vanished during his reign, art was the lesser of wizardry, and people were flagrantly oppressed. Zahhak imprisoned Jamshid's two daughters, Shahrnaz and Arnavaz, and tried to teach them villainy. Two righteous men named Armayel and Garmayel began working in Zahhak's kitchen. They were tasked with preparing two young brains for the snakes daily but decided to free one and feed Zahhak's serpents sheep brains. Then, they would quietly send the young man out into the wilderness.

Thirty young men were saved every month. After some time, they were two-hundred living in the wilderness and keeping goats and ewes. Forty years passed; one night, Zahhak dreamed of two elders with many ordinary men bearing cow-shaped maces who had captured him and were taking him to Mount Damavand. He hollered in terror. Arnavaz, who was by his side, soothed him, and Zahhak told her his dream. Arnavaz said, "Gather all the elders and sages to interpret your dream." The king wanted to know who would take his crown.

Astronomers consulted for three days. They feared telling Zahhak, for the king would take their lives regardless if they
told the truth or lied. There was a wise man among them who
said, "There were many kings before you who were taken
by death, and there is no way out. A man named Fereydoun,
who is not yet born, will lay waste to you with a cow-shaped
mace. "Why does he seek my oblivion?" Asked Zahhak. "He
will avenge his father," said the sage, "He will also drink the
milk of a cow called Barmayeh that you will kill." Zahhak
collapsed from his throne and lost consciousness. For years,
he became restless and wished to kill Fereydoun.

Finally, Fereydoun was born. Zahhak sought Fereydoun
everywhere and killed all infant boys. At last, his soldiers
went to his father Abtin's house, and arrested and killed him.
Fereydoun's mother, Faranak, took the baby to a meadow
with an exceptional cow named Barmayeh; and asked the
grassland keep to tend to his son. The guard agreed. For three
years, Fereydoun drank from the cow's milk and flourished.
Then, Faranak realized that Zahhak had knowledge of the
cow's place. She, therefore, took her son from the meadows
and entrusted him to mobads at the top of Mt. Damavand.
Zahhak went to the grassland with his soldiers, and killed the
cow and the guard. He searched the meadows for Fereydoun,
didn't find him, and set everywhere on fire.

Fereydoun lived in Mt. Alborz for sixteen years. One day, he saw his mother and asked about his father. Faranak said, "Zahhak's soldiers took your father by force, and his brain was fed to Zahhak's snakes." Fereydoun knew that Zahhak's demise was in his hands. He was devastated, for he wanted vengeance, but his mother stopped him. Zahhak dreaded Fereydoun, and forced the elders to write a text about his good deeds. They did as he commanded. Then, they called the people who were wronged to plead for justice.

# Kaveh the Blacksmith

The Blacksmith Kaveh entered the palace and said, "All of my sons were fed to your snakes, and my last son was taken today." The lieutenant-general ordered to free his son, and asked him to sign the letter proclaiming Zahhak's justness in return, but he disobeyed, and left the palace with his son. Kaveh gathered a crowd, put his leather robes on a spear, and said, "Those who are friends of Fereydoun and enemies of Zahhak, join me." Many joined him, and they went to look for Fereydoun. Finally, they reached a mountain and found Fereydoun (Since then, whoever became king, adorned that leather hide with gold and jewels, and named it Derafsh Kaviani). Fereydoun went to his mother, saw his two brothers, Kianush and Shaadkaam, and wished them happiness. Then, he ordered blacksmiths to make a cow-tipped mace in memory of Barmayeh, which had fed him for three years. Fereydoun and his brother departed with a large army commanded by Kaveh.

Fereydoun reached Arvandrud, and asked the guard to take him and his army to the other side. But the guard ignored him and refused to surrender. Fereydoun fumed, and went into the water with his steed. The soldiers followed him into the river, crossed it, and headed to modern-day Baghdad. They did not find Zahhak in his palace, and Fereydoun entered with his horse. Zahhak protected himself with witchcraft and his palace from demons. Fereydoun smashed them all with his mace, and sat on Zahhak's throne. He freed all the women in

Zahhak's harem and guided them on the righteous path of God. Jamshid's daughters came and saluted him. Fereydoun told them his story, and Arnavaz and Shahrnaz rejoiced. Fereydoun asked them to reveal Zahhak's whereabouts. They said that he had escaped to India. They then told him all the injustices he had wrought against the people, his dream, and its interpretation by sages, and said, "He doesn't stay still, for he is tormented by the snakes. Now is the time for him to return."

When Zahhak wasn't in his palace, a rich man named Kondro entered and started to praise Fereydoun. Fereydoun asked questions, and he answered. Then, they threw a feast and received Fereydoun. Kondro left the palace, went to Zahhak, and told him everything he had seen, saying, "There is no hope for your return." Zahhak raged and dishonored him before leaving. Then, he headed for his palace with an army of demons, and entered the palace with a detour. Fereydoun's army immediately assembled before him, and wrestled with each other. The people of the city were fed up with Zahhak, and threw rocks at his soldiers from rooftops. The mobads announced their support for Fereydoun.

Zahhak climbed the palace veranda, and saw Shahrnaz alongside Fereydoun, cursing Zahhak. He envied Fereydoun, took a blade, and went in to kill Shahrnaz.

Fereydoun came forth, and smashed his head with his cow-tipped mace. Soroush said, "It is not yet time for him to die, and you should imprison him in Mt. Damavand." Fereydoun hogtied him and imprisoned him in Mt. Damavand. He then sat on the throne, and gave thanks to God.

# Fereydoun

Fereydoun freed the world from evil, and the people returned to monotheism. The elders gathered around in the month of Mehr and celebrated. They kindled a fire and burned scented substances. This festival, known as Mehregan, lives on to this day. He lived for five-hundred years, and did not do evil for one day. When Fereydoun sat on the throne, Faranak was unaware of everything. One day, her eldest son went to her and informed her that Fereydoun had become king. His mother thanked God, and gave coins to the destitute. Then, she celebrated with the elders, and loaded her treasures on a camel and sent them to his son. The heads of state came to the capital from around the world. Fereydoun left with his army, and vanquished all the evil he saw. He departed Amol to Tammisha.

By the time he was fifty, he had three sons who were all like him. Fereydoun dispatched one of his advisors, Jandal, to whom he was closer and more empathetic than anyone, to find three daughters for his sons from one family. Jandal traversed all countries, and discovered that the king of Yemen had able and virtuous daughters. He went to him and proposed to his daughters. The king of Yemen was vexed. He immediately gathered around the elders of his country for consultation, who said, "If you do not consent to this union, ask them something of which they are incapable. In our view, however, they are competent and great princes." The king arose, called Jandal, and said, "If you want my daughters, you have to send the three princes here so that I may see them; and then, I will marry my daughters according to our customs."

Jandal returned to Iran and relayed the king's demand to Fereydoun, "The king of Yemen has no son and her daughters will succeed him; so, he wants to be certain who their husbands will be." Fereydoun agreed, and accentuated to his sons to speak with logic and wisdom, and think of nothing but chastity and honesty. Fereydoun's three sons were groomed and departed with an army accompanied by mobads. The king of Yemen sent his elders and army to welcome them, held a magnificent ceremony, and wed his three daughters to Fereydoun's sons. They returned to Iran, and Fereydoun divided his territory between his sons. He bestowed Rome and the western nations to Salm, gave the land of the Turks and China to Tur, and gave Iran to Iraj. Then, he sent them off to their nations with a massive army.

A long time later, Fereydoun became frail and his sons became arrogant. It was Salm who became egotistical first, for he was dissatisfied with his share. He sent a messenger to Tur to express his grievance. He was able to persuade Tur to his side, and they met. They sent the wisest mobad to Fereydoun to ask him to reconsider the division of the territories. They expressed, "If you refuse, we will invade and destroy Iraj." The mobad went to Fereydoun's palace, and the king received them warmly. Upon seeing Fereydoun's kindness and grace, the mobad apologized for the message he had brought. Fereydoun was sorrowful to hear his message, and replied, "Tell them that my intention was to divide this vast domain, entrusted to me, among my three dearest sons. But I never consented to separate these parts. You are the kings to three united lands, and your countries have no difference. Therefore, do not associate with the demon of greed, and think of the eternal abode. My death is near, and now is not the time for enmity and war. Know that we are all destined to die, and the world has seen many like you."

## The Iraj death

The mobad received his message and hastened back. After the messenger departed, the father went to Iraj, discussed the matter, and asked him to act preemptively. "If we are all destined to leave this world," said Iraj, "there is no cause for evildoing. With your permission, I shall go to them without an army and a crown, and win their favor." Fereydoun said, "They seek war, and you want a fete and conversation? Indeed, I expected nothing else from you, but are you sure that you will find what you seek this way? Then, take several people with you, for I want to see you back in health." Fereydoun wrote a letter to Salm and Tur, counseled them, and said, "I want you to be at peace. The brother to whom you showed envy is here to comfort you. He is younger than you, and showing sympathy toward him is your duty. Host him for several days, and send him back to me." They sealed the letter, and several elders accompanied Iraj. Iraj came to them, and his brothers came to welcome them. When they saw Iraj, the army noticed that he was worthy of the throne. They all whispered to each other; Salm realized this, and was desolated.

He confided in Tur, "After this, my army and yours consider only Iraj, the king. If we do not vanquish him, we will be vanquished." They pondered all night. The next morning, they woke up and took Iraj into a room to say, "We are older than you. Why should my brother and I suffer in Rome and China while you hold the Kayanian throne? With this act, our father gave his entire wealth to you." "Brother!" responded Iraj, "I don't want the kingdoms Iran, Rome, or China. A king with a repulsive end is no king. We will all rest in a tomb at last. I do not want to see you miserable." Tur was displeased with Iraj, and arose and attacked him. "I shall forgo the throne for your sake," said Iraj, "and shall sit in a corner. I will work and earn a provision." Tur didn't listen to him, and tore his body with his blade. Then, he cut off his head and sent it back to Fereydoun, and they returned to their nations.

Fereydoun waited, and a golden coffin entered the palace. They put Iraj's head before Fereydoun, and he was weeping and whimpering. Upon seeing this sight, Fereydoun collapsed from his horse, and the army tore up their robes. He embraced Iraj's head, and prayed for a descendant of his to take vengeance against his brothers. The entire nation of Iran was clad in black and mourned the loss of Iraj. Some time passed. The news came to Fereydoun that Mahafarid was pregnant with Iraj. After nine months, Mahafarid gave birth to a beautiful girl who closely resembled Iraj. The child grew up, and it was time for her to marry. Fereydoun wed her to a young man named Pashang, and he fathered a handsome son exactly like

Iraj. He was taken to Fereydoun immediately. He thanked the Lord, and named him Manuchehr. Fereydoun nurtured Manuchehr, taught him all there was to know, and spared no efforts. When he grew up, he named him the king of Iran. A vengeful army gathered around him, and Salm and Tur were informed that Manuchehr's presence enlivened Iran's throne. They sent a messenger to Fereydoun to apologize and ask for forgiveness. They asked their father to send Manuchehr to him so that they may bestow upon him a precious treasure.

The messenger came to the king, saluted him, and delivered Salm's and Tur's message. Fereydoun paid no mind to their worthless words, and fired back, "I have not forgotten the day when you sent back Iraj's head to me in a casket. Now it's Manuchehr. Know that it is time you paid for what you did to Iraj." His decisiveness chilled the messenger, and immediately went to Salm and Tur. They prepared two royal courts and a seat for Manuchehr, and waited for his arrival. The messenger told them what he had seen and heard, and said, "Manuchehr intends to spill your blood to avenge his grandfather." They were ill at ease, and contemplated preparing for battle.

They assembled an army, and approached Iran. Fereydoun became aware, and asked Manuchehr to send his army to the Hamund Plain. Hamund teemed with soldiers; all thinking of avenging Iraj. The two armies faced off. A war ensured, and a sea of blood flowed, and Manuchehr was victorious. The next day, no soldier from Salm's and Tur's armies came to fight.

Salm and Tur decided to ambush Manuchehr in the dead of night. Manuchehr's spies were informed, and gave the news to Manuchehr. At night, Tur came to Manuchehr's tent with a hundred-thousand soldiers, and saw a fearsome army. The fighting began, and Manuchehr threw a spear at Tur from behind, and put him down. He decapitated him at once, and informed Fereydoun with a letter. Fereydoun was upset and wept over the death of Tur. News reached Salm, and he decided against fighting and returned. Qaren, the commander of Manuchehr's army, asked the king for permission to chase Salm. He then took an army to Salm's castle, showed Tur's seal, and entered.

At night, he raised Manuchehr's flag, and asked the soldiers to enter the castle. They killed most of Tur's soldiers, but Salm managed to escape to the sea to board a ship, but he saw none. He was fleeing on horseback, but Qaren galloped from behind, caught up to him, and parted his head from his body. Salm's army dispersed. The elders and the army came to Manuchehr, and received promotions. Then, he returned to Fereydoun in Tamisha, who gave him the throne. After some time, Fereydoun entrusted Manuchehr to Saam, Rostam's grandfather, and died with his noble name. According to the tradition of kings, Manuchehr built a tomb and buried Fereydoun in an ebony coffin.

# Manuchehr

Manuchehr mourned Fereydoun for an entire week, and seized the throne on the eighth day. All heroes praised his justice and pledged their support to him. Saam arose and said, "You are the best king of kings Iran has ever seen. From now on, you shall rule Iran, so be merry, for my strongmen and I will rid Iran of evil. Fereydoun promoted me, and asked me to be in your service."

Manuchehr gave him masses of wealth, and Saam and his strong men left the palace. Saam's stunningly handsome son was born in a few days but was an albino. No one had the courage to tell Saam. Finally, the child's nurse informed him of his birth. Saam immediately went to his son, shaken to see his white hair, and said, "Lord, if I have transgressed, why do you punish my son? If they ask me about him, what shall I say?" Immediately, he took the baby up a mountain and left him there. There was a Simorgh nest nearby. As the Simorgh spread its wings to fly to find food for its chicks, it heard a baby cry. It raised him in its claws and took him to its nest to feed its chicks. It looked at the baby, and the Lord put his love in its heart and changed its mind. The Simorgh looked after the body as it protected its chicks.

Sometime later, the baby became a fearless man. One night, Saam dreamed of an Indian man who gave him glad tidings that his son was alive. He called the mobads to interpret his dream, and they said, "You need to repent to the Lord for having left behind a helpless child on a mountain. He lives with the grace of God." The next night, Saam dreamed of a handsome strongman with two other men and an army. One man came near, squabbled with him, and said, "You may have left your son, but God protected him." Saam jumped up, and with his army, went to the mountain he had seen in his dream. He spotted a nest at the peak and decided to climb the mountain, but found no way. He prayed and wept to God.

The Simorgh heard him, told Saam's son, and decided to take him to his father. First, it gave him one of its feathers, and said, "At a time of hardship, burn this so that I may rush to your help." It then gave him a ride on its back, and dropped him near Saam. When he saw his son, Saam thanked Simorgh. He asked his son for forgiveness, and dressed him in beautiful robes. They returned to the city with joy, and Manuchehr was elated to hear the news. Nowzar sent his son to congratulate Saam. Saam, and his son Zaal (named Zaal (Persian for albino) for his white hair) went to Manuchehr. Manuchehr sat on the throne. Qaren sat on one side, and Saam sat on the other. Zaal came before the king in expensive robes. Manuchehr was impressed, and called on Saam to no longer bring him harm. Then, he called the sages to look for Zaal's star. They said, "He will become a renowned hero and guard Iran's borders." The king rejoiced, and gave Zaal precious gifts. Manuchehr gave Zaal the entirety of Kabul, Zabol, and India, from the Sea of China to Sindh River, and sent them off. Saam and Zaal kissed the ground, and departed to Zabolestan.

Saam called the elders of Sistan, gave them precious gifts, and said, "By the king's order, I am obliged to go to Mazandaran and Gorgsaran (Gorgan). I entrust my son to you. Honor him so that you may have respite from my rage." Then, he addressed Zaal, "Try to gather heroes and warriors to your side, and seek knowledge." With his army, he headed to Mazandaran for a battle. Zaal accompanied his father for some of the journeys. He embraced him, and returned to Zabolestan. He sat on the throne, called the elders and the mobads, and began acquiring knowledge and wisdom.

He went to Kabul and May, and the people celebrated his arrival. In Kabul, there was an undefeated athlete named Mehrab. He was an extremely wealthy descendant of Zahhak. When he heard of Zaal's arrival, he went to him with gifts. Zaal received him, and they celebrated. Mehrab returned to his palace, for his wife Sindokht and his daughter Rudabeh were waiting for him. Sindokht asked his husband about Zaal. Mehrab responded that he had yet to see a young man as talented as him, and sang Zaal's praises. Rudabeh fell in love with Zaal. He had five maids with whom she consulted, and they said, "You have many suitors. Are you not ashamed of your father to have fallen in love with Zaal?!" Rudabeh fumed and bellowed, "I want none of the kings; only Saam's son deserves me, whether you consider him young or old." The maids realized that her love was serious, and they swore to spare no effort in uniting her with Zaal. Rudabeh rejoiced.

In the month of Farvardin, her maids accompanied her to the river. Zaal happened to be there on a hunt with his army, and saw her and asked his servants, who said that the maids had come from the Palace of Mehrab. Zaal became fond of Rudabeh. They sent people after each other in secret, and asked questions. One day, the guard of the Palace of Mehrab barred them from leaving, and interrogated them. They brought up the excuse of picking flowers in the meadow. The guard said, "Are you not aware that the king of Zabolestan, Zaal, has camped in the meadow? He will destroy you if he sees you." They went to Rudabeh and told her. That day, Zaal was

waiting eagerly, but Rudabeh didn't come. At night, Zaal rode his horse near Mehrab's palace. Rudabeh came to the palace veranda, and hung her long hair down to let Zaal climb up. They met.

Zaal knew that Manuchehr would prevent their union; for Mehrab was a descendant of Zahhak, but he tried to gain his confidence. He therefore consulted with mobads and asked Saam in a letter to go to Manuchehr and persuade him to agree to their marriage. Saam angrily read the letter, and asked the sages to investigate. After their investigation concluded, they said, "These two nobles will produce an offspring who will safeguard Iran's borders." Saam was delighted, and journeyed to Iran's capital to persuade Manuchehr.

A woman was the intermediary between Rudabeh and Zaal. One day, Sindokht saw him and inquired about their relationship. The woman told the story of Rudabeh and Zaal's love. Sindokht talked to Rudabeh, discovering that Saam was her worthiest spouse, but he did not know that neither Manuchehr nor Mehrab would consent to their marriage. Mehrab went to Sindokht, and saw her perturbed. He asked the reason. Sindokht spoke of the love between Zaal and Rudabeh. Mehrab was vexed and reached for his sword to go to Rudabeh's room, and said, "If Manuchehr and Saam hear this, they will attack us and reduce Kabul to rubble." Sindokht said, "Saam knows, and wants to discuss the matter with the king." Mehrab was petrified, but Sindokht comforted him.

Saam penned a letter to Manuchehr to inform him. The king called the mobads, and said, "I dread the birth of a hero who is a descendant of Zahhak. Fereydoun suffered much hardship to kill Zahhak. What shall I do if their infant takes after his mother and becomes an enemy of Iran?" He sent Nowzar to Saam, and they both went to Manuchehr's palace. The king was happy to see Saam return victorious over the demons of Mazandaran, and received him warmly. Saam told him the entire story. Manuchehr asked him to go to Kabul to kill Mehrab and his entire family, and then sack the city. Saam bowed before the king, and went to Kabul with his army.

Mehrab and Zaal were informed. Zaal mounted his steed at once, and went to greet Saam. Saam›s army welcomed Zaal, and sent him to the army commander. Zaal reminded him of all his suffering and the injustices he had seen from his father, and said, "You have come from Mazandaran to burn and destroy my house?!" I stand against you; cut me in half if you wish, but leave Kabul alone." Saam contemplated and said, "I will write the king a letter. If the Lord shows you benefaction, the king will consent to this marriage." In his letter, he recounted his services to Manuchehr, and asked him to grant Zaal an audience and hear his demand. He noted, "If you make him happy, he will protect Iran›s borders. I cannot forgo his desire. He would rather get slain than see me attack Kabul. If he is acting madly, it is normal, for the Simorgh raises him. I want you to treat him as you see fit."

Zaal took the letter and hastened to the capital. Mehrab was anxious to hear about Saam›s attack. He called Sindokht and directed all of his rage against her, "I cannot resist the onslaught by the king of the world. Therefore, I shall take you and your daughter to the city square and kill you in disgrace. Perhaps, this will bring peace to the king of Iran and he refrains from attacking Kabul." Sindokht responded, "If you fear for your life, wait for the sun to rise. There is another way." "Say what you know," said Mehrab, "Otherwise, wear a blood-stained chador." "I will go to Saam with treasure," said Sindokht, "and I shall persuade him." Mehrab gave her a chest to take to Saam to prevent war and bloodshed. She arrived at Saam's camp, and put the gifts before his feet. Saam was surprised to see a woman sent to him. He knew that accepting the gifts would enrage the king of Iran. Therefore, he sent the gifts to Zaal to take them to Manuchehr.

After she saw that the gifts were accepted, Sindokht said, "If Mehrab is guilty, why do you wish to burn innocent people and the city of Kabul with him? The people are fond of you." "Where did Zaal meet Rudabeh?" asked Saam, "Tell me immediately." Sindokht made Saam vow to bring no harm to her or Rudabeh, then told him the story between the two. Saam realized that Rudabeh was a worthy wife to his son Zaal. Therefore, he recounted the letter and Zaal's presence to Sindokht before Manuchehr. Sindokht was delighted to hear it, and sent a messenger to give glad tiding to Mehrab. The next day, Sindokht journeyed to Kabul with Saam's letter of friendship and precious gifts.

Zaal appeared before the king of Iran, and entered the palace. The king greeted him honorably, then read Saam's letter.

Manuchehr laughed and said, "You brought me tremendous pain. But with Saam's letter telling me his heartache, although I am not happy, I give my consent." Manuchehr called sages to investigate again. After three days, they said that Rudabeh and Zaal would bring a great, noble, and exceptional athlete. Then, Manuchehr called Zaal to be questioned by the mobads to test his intelligence. Zaal pondered briefly, and then gave reasonable answers to all. The king was delighted and gave him precious clothes and gifts. He then replied to Saam's letter, and allowed Zaal and Rudabeh's marriage to proceed.

Zaal sent a messenger to Mehrab. Mehrab joyously called Sindokht, and informed her of Rudabeh's marriage. Rudabeh thanked her mother for her sacrifice. By the king's order, the entire palace of Mehrab was decorated, and Rudabeh prepared for the wedding ceremony. The people celebrated and danced. Zaal went to Saam, and delivered the king's letter. Saam was elated to hear Manuchehr's praise of Zaal and his consent to their marriage. Saam sent a messenger to Mehrab, and announced his own consent. Kabulistan teemed with joy.

Mehrab adorned his army with ornaments and went to Saam. The Hero of the World embraced him, and they went to Kabul with Zaal and Saam. Sindokht took them to a palace where Rudabeh was. They sat upon a golden seat, and solemnized their marriage according to tradition. They celebrated for a week, then Rudabeh, her family, and Zaal headed to Sistan. Saam departed to Mazandaran and Gorgan.

# Rostam's Birth

After some time, Rudabeh went into labor. The baby was so enormous that he could not leave his mother's womb. Rudabeh wrestled with death, and Sindokht clawed her own hair and face. Suddenly, Zaal remembered Simorgh. He burnt its feather, and it appeared in moments. Zaal expressed his problem, and Simorgh said, "First, intoxicate Rudabeh, then pierce her side with a blade, take the baby, and stitch her back up." Zaal called a skilled physician, and the baby was born. He then rubbed Simorgh's feather on the wound for a quick recovery. Simorgh left another feather, and then flew away.

The baby was as substantial as an elephant calf. Rudabeh slept for days and felt no pain. When she regained consciousness, the baby was brought to her. Rudabeh smiled when she saw him. They named him Rostam, and drew a likeness of him and sent it to Saam. There was a celebration across all of Zabol and Kabul. Saam gave the messenger many coins, and held a majestic ceremony. He thanked God, and asked Zaal to nurture the child carefully. Ten nurses would feed Rostam milk, but he would still be hungry. In the end, they would fill him up with bread and meat. He would eat as much as five men. At the age of eight, he was a mature young man. When he heard the praise of Rostam, Saam gathered his army and headed to Zabolestan.

Zaal and Mehrab welcomed him warmly. Rostam came to Saam on the back of an elephant. He kissed his grandfather's throne and welcomed him. Saam embraced and kissed him, and stayed with him for a month. One day when Mehrab was extremely drunk, he looked at Rostam and said, "I do not fear Zaal, Rostam, or the king. Rostam and I will become one. I shall revive Zahhak's tradition, and no one can stop me. Zaal and Saam laughed. Saam left them in a month and said, "I think my death is near. Do not forget my advices, and never stray from the righteous path." He then said goodbye to his two sons and left.

At that moment, Manuchehr was a hundred and twenty. The sages announced that he would die. He sat on the Kayanian throne, called the elders and mobads, and revealed his secrets. Then, he called his son Nowzar and counseled him, "I took Iraj's vengeance upon Salm and Tur, and rid the world of evil. After so many years, it seems I have not seen anything from the world. I leave the throne and crown to you, just as they were entrusted to me by Fereydoun. Do not tread on any other path but the righteous one, and only worship the Lord. Moses is God's prophet; make sure not to be his enemy. Seek help from Zaal and Saam in war, and from Zaal's son, who is still a child." He then closed his eyes, and died peacefully. Nowzar shed many tears for him.

# Nowzar

After mourning his father's passing, Nowzar assumed the throne. Shortly afterward, Nowzar fell in love with treasure and riches, and forgot the people. The people rebelled. Nowzar sent someone after Saam, and said, "Manuchehr praised Saam even on his deathbed. You are my only ally, a hero and the king's lover. You look after Iran, and now the country is unruly. They shall pull me down from the throne if you do not wield a mace and rush to my help."

Saam let out a cold sigh. At dawn, he dispatched his army to the capital. The elders greeted him, and complained of Nowzar's oppression. They asked Saam to sit on the throne. Saam was troubled and rejected their demand, saying, "He will not continue this state. I will guide him back to the righteous path, and you will regret your action." The elders bowed their heads in shame, and then went to Nowzar. Saam counseled him, and spoke a lot about Fereydoun, Manuchehr, and Hushang. Nowzar listened to him, and did as he wished. He then bestowed upon Saam precious gifts, and Saam returned to his city.

## The Iran-Turan War

Some time passed. Manuchehr's death became news in Turan, and King Pashang decided to attack Iran and avenge his father's blood, Tur. He called Arjasp, Garsivaz, Barman, Viseh, and his army commanders. He also asked for his son, Afrasiab, and told him the story of Tur and Salm. Afrasiab volunteered to fight the Iranians, and Pashang was pleased with his son's bravery. As news of the war spread around the palace, Agrirath, Pashang's other son, reminded him that fighting Saam, Garshasp, and Qaren was impossible. "It is better if we do not rebel," he said. Pashang, thinking that he could depend on Afrasiab, made up an excuse and asked him to accompany his brother.

It was springtime. Turan assembled a massive army from China, Turkey, and the Far East, and reached near Jeyhun River. Nowzar was notified of Turan's assault. Heimmediatelyprepared his army and sent them to Hamun. Qaren was Nowzar's commander, and they camped near a village. Afrasiab chose Shamasas and Khazravan as his commanders, and entrusted the army to them. At that time, news reached that Saam has passed away, and Zaal needs to prepare a tomb for him. Afrasiab was ecstatic. His army was endless, and before him was Nowzar's army of 140,000. Afrasiab penned a letter to Pashang, "Saam died and Zaal is burying his father, and they are unable to fight. Now, Shamasas will go to Sistan with an army of thirty-thousand to take Zaal's throne.

At dawn, the two armies faced off in Gorgan. Barman (Viseh's son) went to Afrasiab and asked for his order to go to war. Agrirath said, "If you are slain, our army will be demoralized. We should send an unknown hero to the field." Afrasiab was vexed, and ordered Barman to be sent to the battlefield. He sought challengers. Nobody from Qaren's army volunteered to fight, except Qobad the Courageous, who was an old man. Qobad was ready for war, and, eventually, death, and he went into the field and faced Barman. They fought each other from dawn until night. At last, Barman struck Qobad's hip with a brick and killed him. Then, he went after Afrasiab, and gave him the good news. Qaren saw Qobad's death (his brother) and ordered his army to attack. The two armies clashed, and many were killed on both sides. The darkness of night descended. Qaren directed the army toward the village, near Nowzar's camp, and notified him of Qobad's death.

On the second day, the two armies fought again, and a river of blood flowed. The soldiers tussled, and the earth became red. The Iranian army suffered more deaths. Nowzar felt that the fate of his kingdom was uncertain. Then, he called his two sons, Tous and Gostaham, wept in Manuchehr's memory, and said, "Without notifying the army, go to Pars, take your children, and send them to Mount Alborz. Then, prepare the army's provision, and if I am killed, two descendants of Fereydoun must survive to assume the kingdom in the promised day." They both left.

After two days, the two armies reposed. On the third day, Afrasiab's army prepared for battle. Qaren created a column at the heart of his army against the enemy. Taliman, the Hero, at the left, and Shapur, at the king's right prepared for battle, and fought until sunset. Most of Shapur's army was destroyed, and so was he. The Turks directed their attack at the village. Afrasiab sent Viseh to Pars with an army topreventprovisions from reaching the Iranian army. Qaren came to Nowzar enraged, and asked him to order him to go to Pars and resist Viseh's army. Nowzar said, "Tous and Gostaham have already been sent on this mission, and Iran's army needs Qaren more than ever. Qaren knew that if Afrasiab's army took the soldiers' wives in Pars captive, no one would be willing to fight; then, at midnight, he consulted his heroes and prepared to go to Pars.

On the other side, Barman and his army were waiting for provision for Iranians. Qaren was eager to avenge his brothers, and wrestled him. He immediately pierced his side with a spear and killed him. Barman's army dispersed. Nowzar was anxious to find out that Qaren had headed to Pars, and fearing for his life, followed him. Afrasiab heard the news, gathered his army, and pursued him relentlessly. He managed to capture Nowzar. Afrasiab captured Nowzar and twelve-hundred soldiers. When he realized that Qaren had already left, he called Viseh to follow Qaren, and avenge his son, Barman. Viseh followed Qaren with a vast army. On the way, he saw the corpses of his son and many of Turan's soldiers. He wept for some time, and then continued along until he reached Qaren in Hamun. The two armies lined up against each other, and Viseh told Qaren, "The king of Iran is captured, and we control the entire realm of Iran." Qaren responded, "I killed your son to avenge my brother, and now is your turn, so that I may vacate the earth of your existence." The war started, and Viseh and Qaren fought. Finally, fate turned its back to Viseh, and he was defeated.

Viseh fled at once, but Qaren didn't chase him. Viseh went to Afrasiab and wept for her son's demise, while Shamasas headed for Sistan. Khazravan and thirty-thousand swordsmen accompanied him. They reached River Hirmand as Zaal was burying Saam, and Mehrab the Hero was in the city. He spotted Turan's army, sent a smooth-talking messenger to Shamasas, and said, "We are descendants of Zahhak, and we resent Nowzar's rule. I joined the King of Iran to save myself; for I was left with no choice. Now, I control the city, the throne, and the people of Zabolestan. Zaal is burying Saam, and I am rejoicing. I can serve Afrasiab if so, he demands."

He comforted Shamasas with this thought. Then, he sent a brave man to Zaal to deliver his message, "Return to Zabol as soon as possible for two heroes from Turan and an endless army have camped near River Hirmand. I stopped their attack against the city." After receiving the message, Zaal immediately returned to Mehrab. He held his bow, and aimed three arrows toward Turan's army at night. At dawn, the soldiers saw the arrows and realized that they belonged to Zaal. The drumbeats of war commenced. Zaal had stationed his army around Hamun. The two armies stood against each other. Khazravan, Turan's hero, attacked Zaal, and struck him with a column, shredding his armor. Zaal wore another armor, returned to the battlefield, and smashed Khazravan's head with a mace. Turan's hero died on the spot. Zaal called Shamasas to the battlefield, but he hid in cowardice. Zaal caught a glimpse of Kolbad, another Turan hero, attacked him with his mace, and fled. In the blink of an eye, Zaal's arrow struck him. Shamasas immediately fled, and his army dispersed. A severe fighting ensued, and Zabolestan's army chased Turan's army.

Shamasas came across Qaren on the way, and his exhausted army entered another fight. In the end, Shamasas and some of his soldiers managed to escape, but his army was routed. The spies informed Pashang that two of Turan's heroes were dead. He erupted, and ordered to bring Nowzar and savagely have his head cut off. He also wanted to cut off the other heroes' heads, but Agrirath stopped him and asked the king to detain them. Then, he sent them to Sari in shackles. Afrasiab ventured to the village of Rey and conquered it. Gostaham and Tous heard the news, went to Zaal, and asked him to avenge the blood of their father, Nowzar, from Turan. Zaal comforted them, saying, "We are all destined to die one day." He sent Kashvad to fight Agrirath and release the Iranian heads of state. Agrirath said, "I shall deliver the commanders of the

Iranian army in Sari without war and bloodshed. But I need to find a way not to make an enemy of my brother, and not start a fight with Zaal."

Afterwards, Agrirath delivered the elders in Sari, and then departed to Rey. Kashvad released the elders from chains and took them to Zaal on horses. Zaal wept for their plight, and bestowed upon them a fitting position and wealth. Afrasiab was notified of the Iranian elders' escape, and asked Agrirath, "What have you done? I told you to kill them. Are you in full possession of your faculties?!" "Think of the Lord whenever you can do wrong to someone," said Agrirath, "Some shame and honor go a long way." Afrasiab was furious, and split Agrirath in half with his sword. Zaal was informed of Agrirath's death, and was grief-stricken. He was livid, and set off to Pars to avenge him. A massive army accompanied him. The news came to Afrasiab, and he moved his army to Rey. The two armies battled with many dead on both sides.

## Zou Tahmasp

Zaal assembled renowned Iranian heroes and asked them to find a descendant of Fereydoun worthy of the Iranian throne, for he considered Tous and Gostaham undeserving. They looked for a long time, and found an eighty-year-old man named Zou Tahmasp, who was very charitable and faithful. He sat upon the Iranian throne for five years, and prevented wrongdoing by the army. There was a drought during his rule, but the people did not suffer. For eight months, the armies of Iran and Turan were ready for battle. They realized that their savagery caused the drought . Therefore, the elders gathered around, and divided the lands. Then, Tahmasp went to Pars, and Zaal went to Zabol. What followed was a rain that brought an end to the drought.

Zou Tahmasp died, and his son Garshasp succeeded him. Afrasiab attacked Iran again. The elders went to Zaal and complained that he was failing to protect Iranian soil. "I have grown frail," said Zaal, "and I am unable to fight. Rostam can replace me, but he needs a suitable ride." By Zaal's order, they searched all horse teams to find one for Rostam, but none could withstand his weight. Rostam sat on a hill and watched the horses brought in from Kabul. Suddenly, he saw a swift and beautiful mare. He went to the team keeper and asked about the animal. The horsekeeper warned him that the mare was very sensitive about her three-year-old colt (Rakhsh), and would attack him.

Rostam threw a lasso and held the mare, which thereby attacked Rostam. Rostam roared so ferociously that she fled into the middle of the team; and he mounted Rakhsh, and noticed that the animal's back would not bend under his weight. He asked its price, and the horsekeeper said, "The price of this horse is the emancipation of Iran's borders." Rostam laughed and left. Zaal gave him the mace of his father, Saam. The horse was branded with Rostam's name, who led a huge army, and Zaal, an old man, followed him. Then, Garshasp died as well; and when the news was brought to Afrasiab, he moved his army to Rey.

Zaal asked the elders to enthrone Kayqubad, a descendant of Fereydoun. Zaal addressed Rostam, "Go to Mt. Alborz and bring Kayqubad to the capital with an army. You need to accomplish this in two weeks." The nation of Turan was notified, and they closed the road to Rostam. He fought them, and Turan's heroes fled. They went to Afrasiab, and told him the entire story. Afrasiab called Qalon (Turkic hero), and ordered him to guard the mountain.

Rostam was approaching Mt. Alborz. Within two kilometers, he saw a group assembled near the river under the shade of the trees. A handsome man was seated on the throne, and the heroes beside him stood to serve him. When they saw Rostam and asked him to be his guest. Rostam answered, "Iran is without a king, and I should immediately go to Mt. Alborz. I do not have time for a reception. Point me toward

Kayqubad's location so I may bring him to the capital immediately." The man laughed and said, "I'm Kayqubad." Rostam stepped off his Rakhsh, and bowed before him. They made merry for some time, and Rostam saluted him in the name of Zaal and Iran's elders. Kayqubad said, "One night, I dreamed of two white goshawks carrying a glittering crown, and they put it on my head. I celebrated this dream and awaited your arrival."

They moved and reached Qalon, who blocked their path. Kayqubad decided to fight them, but Rostam stopped and fought them. Qalon attacked him, and Rostam plunged his spear into his body. Qalon's entire army retreated. Rostam went to the meadow with Kayqubad, and took him to Zaal at dawn.

# Kayqubad

Kayqubad became the king of Iran. Zaal, Qaren, Kashvad, Kharad, Borzin, and the heroes of the army bowed before him, and told him of Afrasiab. Kayqubad assembled the army, and prepared to confront Turan. Mehrab was at one side, Gazhdaham was on the other, and Qaren and Kayqubad were at the heart of the army. Rostam led, and Zaal and Kayqubad were at the back. They beat the drums of war, and the soldiers engaged. Qaren spotted Shamasas and killed him with his sword against his head.

After seeing this scene, Rostam was tempted to kill Afrasiab. He came to Zaal and said, "Who is Afrasiab, and where is he in the army? That I may drag him to you, kicking and screaming." Zaal said, "Listen, my son. Avoid fighting him, for he is a male dragon. He is covered with iron from head to toe, and has tied a black cloth to his helmet." "The Lord is on my side," declared Rostam, "and I shall accomplish this with Rakhsh's help." He attacked the heart of Turan's army. "Who is this teenager?" asked Afrasiab. After seeing him, Rostam raised his mace and rushed toward him. He killed many soldiers, and brought himself to Afrasiab. He snatched him by the belt and lifted him off his horse. Luckily for Afrasiab, the belt opened and he fell down. Soldiers surrounded him and dragged him away. Rostam regretted not holding onto something stronger. Kayqubad heard this, rejoiced, and attacked Turan's army.

Afrasiab fled Jeyhun to Pashang, saying, "You were the main culprit of this war. You dishonored your treaty with the king of Iran, and were hellbent on wiping Fereydoun's descendants from the face of the earth." He then recounted Rostam's fighting, and said, "Despite all of my might, I am but a fly in his hands. You should have been satisfied with Fereydoun's demarcation and not sought Tur's vengeance. War with Iran was a game to you, and you failed to see how heroes such as Qobad, Kalbad, Barman, Khazravan, and Shamasas would be slain. Worst of all, we cannot retaliate after this humiliation. You should make peace with Kayqubad now, for he commands heroes such as Rostam, Qaren, Kashvad, Mehrab and Zaal-e-Dastan.

Pashang was stunned. He wrote a letter to Kayqubad, and sent a groveling messenger to Iran. In his letter, he had stated that they would refrain from taking revenge, and would be satisfied with Fereydoun's demarcation. The Iranians responded that they were the ones who started the war and bloodshed, and if they respected their covenant and Fereydoun's demarcation, Iran would refrain from war. The messenger returned to Pashang with the response, and his army retreated. Rostam told Kayqubad, "O King of Kings, do not make peace with him. I shall be a nightmare for them." Kayqubad responded, "There is nothing greater than peace in this world. He is of my blood, and I do not wish to keep fighting him."

Then, Kayqubad put to Rostam's name the territory spanning Zabolestan to the Indus River, and asked him to return to his land. Mehrab returned to Kabul. He then gave Zaal, Qaren, Kashvad, Barzin, and Kharrad precious gifts. Kayqubad headed to Estakhr in Pars, assumed the throne, and helped the poor and the oppressed with a decree. He ruled for one-hundred years, and had four wise sons, Kavus, Kiarash, Kaypashin, and Armin. On his deathbed, he called Kavus, talked to him about justice, and asked him to succeed him. He then advised him, and closed his eyes to the world.

# Kay Kavus

Kavus became the ruler of Iran, and the entire world obeyed him. His treasury was majestic, and he was grander than all the kings that preceded him. He was on the throne one day, and his heroes were granted an audience. An instrumentalist demon from Mazandaran asked the guards to be allowed in. He started to play and sing a song in Mazanderani. Kavus heard the poem and was tempted to move there with his army. He told his heroes, "I am greater than Jamshid, Zahhak, and Kayqubad. I want to see the world. The elders disagreed, but no one dared to oppose him.

They gathered around to come up with a solution and to repel this terrible fate from Iran. They sent a messenger to Zaal to say, "O hero of Iran, the king is tempted to conquer Mazandaran. If we lose time, he will go and all of your efforts will have been for naught." Zaal trembled like a tree and said, "I shall go to him and counsel him, but I fear he will not heed my advice."

The elders welcomed him, and went to the king. Zaal advised him and asked him to follow the tradition of previous kings. Kavus said, "I'm braver than the previous kings. I want to remove their demons and undo their spells." After Kavus insisted, Zaal gave in and headed to Sistan. The king departed to Mazandaran with great heroes, and entrusted the throne to Milad, saying, "If you have any problems, tell Zaal and Rostam." By the king›s order, Giv selected heroes for the king's army, and they sacked the city of Mazandaran. They witnessed a paradisaical city, and plundered everything within a week. The king of Mazandaran informed the White Demon and sough help. The White Demon brought his army and prepared to assist him. At night, a black cloud shrouded the sky, rained stones, and destroyed much of the Iranian army. By dawn, half of the army and Kavus had been blinded.

The demons plundered all of its wealth, and took Kavus and the heroes captive. The White Demon assigned twelve-thousand warrior demons commanded by Arjhang to guard the Iranians, and entrusted all the treasure to it. Kavus, a captive, sent some of his men outside the prison to go to Zaal in secret, give him the bitter news, and seek help. He regretted that he didn't heed Zaal's advice, and asked him to come to his aid as fast as possible.

Zaal was desolated, kept it a secret from everyone, and told Rostam, "The demons captured the king of Iran. You need to ride Rakhsh and go for his help. You need to vanquish Arjhang and the White Demon." "The road is long," said Rostam, "and how would I go from Zabolestan to Mazandaran?" "There are two ways to Mazandaran," said Zaal, "One is the path taken by Kavus, which is longer. The other is shorter, and scattered with demons, lions, and darkness. May the Lord be with you." "I will leave neither Arjhang, nor the White Demon, nor Sanjeh, nor Bid alive, and I shall destroy them in the name of God and with Rakhsh's help." He bid them farewell, and Rudabeh and Dastan sent him off weeping.

## Rostam's Seven Labors

Rostam traversed the journey of two days in one. When he became hungry, he hunted a Zebra. Then, he left Rakhsh and reclined on the reed bed. He would then start his journey to the Seven Labors.

**The First Labor:** An enormous lion approached him early into the night. The lion tried to attack Rakhsh, but the horse smashed its head with its two hooves, and held its back in its teeth. It pounded it into to ground until it was torn apart. When Rostam woke up, he found the lion dead. "You should not have fought the lion alone!" said Rostam, "You should have woken me up to fight it, and you would have stayed away." He thanked God.

**The Second Labor:** Rostam reached a scorching hot desert and dismounted his horse. Rostam and Rakhsh were both extremely thirsty, and Rostam collapsed to the ground and whispered God's name. An ewe passed in front of him, which he knew was sent by God. He followed it, and reached a spring and took his robes. They both drank some water, and Rostam thanked God. He washed himself and his clothes and hunted a nearby zebra. He then slept, and instructed Rakhsh to wake him up in the event of an approaching demon or lion without fighting.

**The Third Labor:** Rostam reached a hill and dwelling-place of a mighty dragon. No animal, demon, or lion would dare go near. Rostam was asleep, and the dragon got near. It saw him and pondered, "Who dares sleep near here?!" Rakhsh spotted it, and pounded its hoof to the ground. Rostam woke up, but the dragon hid himself. Rostam thought that Rakhsh had woken him up nonsensically. He raged, screamed at it, and went back to sleep.

Once again, the dragon approached, and Rakhsh woke Rostam up as before; but the dragon disappeared again. Rostam roamed the entire desert but saw nothing. He was furious, and hollered at Rakhsh and said, "If you wake me up without reason again, I shall put your head to the sword, and go to Mazandaran on foot." He slept for the third time. The dragon breathed fire. Rakhsh was frightened, but could neither wake up Rostam nor confront the dragon. At last, it threw caution to the wind, went to Rostam, and woke him up. Rostam was angry, but before he screamed, God willed for the dragon to remain visible, and he saw it. He immediately unsheathed his sword, attacked it, and Rakhsh bit and tore apart its back. Rostam immediately cut off its head, and the dragon's warm blood streamed on the ground. Rostam washed himself up and thanked God.

**The Fourth Labor:** After he finished praying to the Lord, Rostam mounted his steed, and headed to the land of the wizard. He took a long journey, and reached a lush area near Juybar. The old wizard was given a banquet filled with food. When Rostam arrived, the wizard hid. Rostam sat next to the banquet jovially and ate. He then started to sing, and the sorcerer heard him. She turned herself into a beautiful girl, and came to Rostam. Rostam prayed to God, and as he continued, the sorcerer could not bear the Lord's name and turned back into the old woman. Rostam immediately snatched her with a lasso, and split her in half with his dagger.

**The Fifth Labor:** Rostam set forth again and reached the land of darkness. He could see nothing, and released Rakhsh's rein. Rakhsh took him to the land of light, and he sweltered. He took off his armor, left Rakhsh to graze, and slept himself. When the field watcher saw Rakhsh grazing in the grass, he angrily hit its hoof with a stick; Rostam woke up and screamed. He was furious, and pulled his ear until it was torn off. The watchman yelled, and went to the demon Olad to complain. Olad came to the plain and sought Rostam. Upon seeing him, Rostam immediately climbed Rakhsh and introduced himself. He then started slaughtering his soldiers, then threw a lasso and captured Olad. Olad's army all but disappeared, and he told him, "If you tell me the White Demon's whereabouts so that I may free Kavus and Iran's heroes, I shall appoint you as the king of Mazandaran." Olad said, "I'll do as you say, don't take my life in vain. The White Demon lives in a fearsome place between two mountains, and has twelve-thousand warriors. Pooladghondi is his commander, and Bid and Senjeh are his guards. He is extremely strong, and you cannot overcome him alone." Rostam scoffed, and said, "If this is true, come with me and gaze upon my abilities. I fight with the power of Yazata, and owe him everything. Then, show me the way."

They journeyed to Mount Esperoz, and reached the city of Mazandaran. There were candles and torches everywhere. Olad said, "This is the residence of Arjhang Div." Rostam tied Olad to a tree, and rode Rakhsh.

**The Sixth Labor:** Rostam attacked Arjhang's army, which emerged from the tent. Rostam charged at him, grabbed his head, separated it from the body, and threw it into the demons' middle, which all vanished at once. He unsheathed his sword, and slew them all. Then, he went after Olad in Mt. Esperoz, untied him, and asked Kavus' whereabouts. Upon entering the city, Rakhsh roared. Rostam asked Kavus' place and was taken to him. Kavus and the other heroes embraced Rostam and asked about the hardships of the path. Kavus said, "If this news reaches the White Demon, he will immediately come here with his army, and all your efforts will have been in vain. You should go after the White Demon, who lives in an eerie cave. My army and I have been blinded, and the physicians say that its cure is three drops of blood from the White Demon's liver."

**The Seventh Labor:** Rostam prepared himself, and headed to Haft Kooh. When he approached the cave, he asked Olad to guide him. Olad said, "Attack them at noon, for the demons sleep early. Thus, you will surely prevail." Rostam waited for the sun to reach the middle of the sky. Then, he tied Olad in ropes, descended upon the demon army like lightning, and struck many of their heads with a sword. The demons all escaped, and no one challenged him. Rostam entered a dark cave, looked around for some time, and saw a black demon with white hair. The demon grabbed a large slate. Rostam panicked, and cut off one leg from the thigh. Blood streamed from the demon's body, and they clashed. Rostam wondered, "If I am done fighting this demon today, I shall live long." "If I am freed from this monster," said the demon, "No one will ever see me in Mazandaran."

 Rostam mentioned the Lord's name, raised the demon with the power of Yazata, and pounded him to the ground. He immediately took out his blade, pierced its side, and removed its liver. He entrusted it to Olad to take it to Kavus and the heroes; then, he returned and cut off the heads of thousands of demons. Kavus was briefed of Rostam's victory and the White Demon's liver. The king and his heroes regained their vision, and people went to greet Rostam. Kavus sat on the throne, and heroes such as Tous, Fariborz, Goudarz, Giv, Roham, Gorgin and Farhad were alongside him. They celebrated for a week, and on the eighth day, they scattered around Mazandaran to hunt demons. Then, Kavus wrote a letter to the king of Mazandaran. He was told, "If you want to remain the ruler of Mazandaran, come kiss the hand of Kavus, and pay your taxes." The king gave the letter to Farhad for delivery. The ruler of Mazandaran received him disrespectfully, responded to Kavus harshly, and considered him inferior.

Farhad returned to Kavus and recounted the events. Kavus discussed the matter with Rostam, who asked the king to write another letter and take it to Mazandaran himself. Kavus gave Rostam full authority, and entrusted the letter to him.

Rostam reached the king of Mazandaran's camp, the messenger introduced him, and several elders welcomed him. Rostam uprooted a tree, hurled it toward Mazandaran's army, and many soldiers were trapped under it. A hero came forward, held Rostam's hand, and pressed it. Rostam scoffed and pressed his hands so hard that he became pale and fell down from his horse. The messenger delivered the news to the king. He sent another hero named Kolahur, who also pressed Rostam's hand, and Rostam pressured him so much that he screamed. He went to the king and counseled him, "We will not fight him, for he is very strong."

Rostam went to the king and gave him the letter. The king fumed after reading it and said, "Tell Kavus that if you are the king of Iran, I am the king of Mazandaran; do not ask me to surrender, for you will regret this." Rostam couldn›t tolerate his words. He immediately returned to Kavus, and told him. Kavus prepared an army and all heroes prepared for battle. A hero named Juyan emerged from Mazandaran's army and sought a challenger, but no one dared to confront him. Rostam went to Kavus and asked permission to fight. Then, he went forward, attacked Juyan, raised his armor with a spear, lifted him from the saddle, and threw him over. The ruler of Mazandaran ordered his soldiers to attack, and the two armies fought for a week. On the eighth day, Kavus wept for the Lord and prayed. The two armies faced off again. Rostam whispered the name of God, and killed many demons and elephants. He spotted the king of Mazandaran, charged at him, and struck him with a spear. With a spell, he turned into a slate.

Rostam stood with the slate for some time; then, Kavus came to him and asked the reason for the delay. Rostam told him everything, and then carried the slate to the Iranian camp. He said, "Either you reveal yourself, or I crush this slate with sword and axe." A tall black demon appeared immediately. Rostam put it in chain, and took it to the king. Kavus called the executioner, ordered it to be smashed to pieces, and sent it back to its camp. Then, he sent heroes to the Mazandaran camp to decapitate all demons, and to bestow status and wealth upon the humans who obeyed him.

Rostam asked Kavus for Olad to be appointed the king of Mazandaran for his services. Kavus put Olad on the throne, and headed to Pars himself. All Iranian rejoiced for his victory and gave him a hero's welcome. The king gave Rostam precious clothes and gifts, put the kingdom of Sistan to his name, and named him the Hero of the World. Rostam kissed Kavus' throne, and went to Zaal in Sistan. Kavus made Tous his grand vizier, put the city of Sepahan to his name, and gave the other heroes of Iran precious presents.

# Sohrab

Early in the morning, Rostam went to the border with Turan on a hunt. He saw a herd of zebras near the border, rejoiced, hunted, and ate one. He released Rakhsh to graze, then took a nap. Eight Turkic riders were passing by and saw Rakhsh and seized it. Rostam woke up, and didn't see Rakhsh anywhere. He was desolated, for he could not return to his city without his horse. Resentfully, he headed toward Samangan, and the king was informed of his arrival. The elders of Turan welcomed him and said, "The people of this city love you, and no one has enmity toward you. We will find and return your horse if you come to the king's palace as a guest."

Rostam agreed and went to the palace. That night, they celebrated and Rostam slept. The door to his room was opened at midnight and a beautiful girl entered. Rostam asked her name. She introduced herself as Tahmina and said, "I am in love with you and want to become your wife so that I may carry your son. If you accept, I will find you Rakhsh." Rostam grew fond of Tahmina. He then called a Mobad and suited to her father. The king was elated to hear the news, and agreed to their marriage.

After some time, Rostam decided to return to his country; and he took the orb from his arms, gave it to Tahmina, and asked her to tie it to their daughter's head or their son›s arm. The king gave Rostam the glad tidings of finding Rakhsh. He was thrilled, and headed to Sistan. Nine months later, Tahmina gave birth to a handsome son. He took after Rostam and Saam, and was named Sohrab. At the age of one, Sohrab was as great as Rostam and Zaal in stature. At the age of three, he would play polo, and at the age of five, he wielded a bow and arrow. At the age of ten, no one could stand against him.

One day, his mother came and he asked of his father. His mother talked of Rostam and his dynasty. Then, she gave her Rostam's letter with his orb. Afrasiab took the opportunity and told him, "If your father finds out, he will take you with him, and your mother will become sorrowful." Sohrab was an egotistical young man and said, "I shall assemble an army in Turan, kick Kavus off the throne, and enthrone Rostam." Very soon, he managed to assemble a massive army, and Afrasiab became jubilant. He sent along twelve-thousand soldiers with Barman and Hooman to accompany Sohrab, and warned them that he was not to know that Sohrab was the son of Rostam. They looked after Sohrab everywhere, and gave him Sohrab's letter, which stated, "If you manage to defeat the Iranian army, I shall make you king, and Iran and Turan will be united." He sent Sohrab many gifts.

They headed to the White Fort, Iran's first line of defense. The guard, Hojir, was a lionheart. Hojir saw the army, and left the fortress alone to fight them. Sohrab was stunned. They fought for a long time; and at last, Sohrab plunged his spear into Hojir's hip, raised him from his horse, and smashed him to the ground. When he attempted to take his head, Hojir begged. Then, Sohrab tied his hands and took him to Hooman.

Gordafarid, the daughter of Gazhdaham, who was a brave horsewoman, put on her armor and left the fortress. She hid her hair under her helmet, mounted her horse, and charged at Sohrab.

She was ashamed of Hojir's begging, and attacked Sohrab like a raging lion. They fought for two to three days, and at last, Sohrab broke her spear and jumped on her horse. He removed her helmet, and was astounded to see that she was a girl. Gordafarid could only think of trickery, and said, "Your army must not know that you took your time fighting a girl. Now, you command the fortress and the army, and I obey you. I shall go to the fort and talk to the elders. Then, I shall open the gates for you." Gordafarid entered the fortress, and the elders were dismayed by her, for she had fought and tricked Sohrab. Gordafarid came to the top of the fortress. He saw Sohrab waiting, and asked, "What are you waiting for?! Return to your army, and know that Turks cannot be spouses to Iranians. If Rostam finds out that you have attacked Iran, he will not leave any of you alive. You should return to Turan, and forget about fighting." When Sohrab realized that he had been bamboozled, he attacked a village near the fortress and plundered it.

Gazhdaham immediately wrote a letter to the King of Iran, and described everything. He said, a twelve-year-old hero attacked us with an army from Turan, and he raised Hojir in the blink of an eye and pounded them into the dirt. He sent the messenger to the capital from the hidden gate, and let people out at night with food and grain. At dawn, Sohrab and his army came to the fort and found it vacated. He entered the fort with his army, and the messenger delivered the letter to Kavus.

The elders and the heroes went to the king for consultation. Kavus ordered to write a letter to Rostam. Then, he gave the letter to Giv to go to Rostam immediately and bring him back. When Giv reached Zabol, Rostam and the elders greeted him. He went to the veranda and read the letter, and they proclaimed that a child resembling Saam had set foot in the universe. Rostam waited and said, "I have a son from the king of Samangan's daughter, but he is still a child and knows nothing of war."

Rostam hosted Giv, and they celebrated for four days. Giv prepared to depart, and asked Rostam to come to the capital as soon as possible, for Kavus was in a frenzy. Rostam and his army headed to the capital, and he and Giv went to Kavus and paid their respects. The king was livid that they were late, and he first screamed at Giv, and then abused Rostam. He ordered Giv to catch Rostam and put a noose around his neck, but he disobeyed him. Kavus was enraged, and ordered Tous to do so. Tous went forward, and held Rostam's hand to take him outside the palace until the king›s rage faded. Rostam struck him so ferociously that he hit the ground head first. Rostam walked over him, and yelled at Kavus, "Put Sohrab to the noose if you are man enough, for he has wreaked havoc throughout Iran." He left the palace for Zabol. The elders were all upset, and they went to Goudarz and asked him to bring peace. Goudarz went to Kavus and said, "Have you forgotten what Rostam has done for you? How are you so hasty to order his execution?!" Kavus swallowed his pride, for he had no one to confront Sohrab. He asked Goudarz to follow Rostam and convince him to return.

Goudarz went to Rostam and reminded him that Kavus was a belligerent and unwise man, and said, "You are the only hope of Iran and her army. If you were troubled by the king, how is the Iranian guilty?" To convince him to return, he asked, "Perhaps you also are scared of Sohrab?" Rostam was affronted, and returned to the palace. The king apologized to him, and a celebration was held. On the next day, Rostam, Giv and Tous headed to the White Fortress. A massive army assembled before the fort. When he saw the might of the Iranian army, Hooman trembled in fear. However, Sohrab ordered to have a feast that night, and to cheer and dance. At night, Rostam came to Kavus and asked him to go to Sohrab's army in secret and gather information. Rostam entered the White Fortress in disguise. He saw Sohrab resting on a seat with Zhenderazm (Sohrab's uncle) on one side and Hooman and Barman on the other. Sohrab had taken up all the space, and was surrounded by servants.

Zhenderazm saw a tall man in the dark. He knew that there was no one of such stature among the Turk heroes; so he stood up, went toward him, and asked, "Who are you? Come to the light at once so that I may see you." Rostam slapped him on the neck, killing him instantly.

After some time, Sohrab noticed that his uncle was absent. He sent someone after him, and they found his inanimate body. He ordered the soldiers to stay awake until morning, and returned to the party to celebrate.

Rostam entered the Iranian camp. Giv (Rostam's groom and husband to Banu Goshasp, Rostam's daughter) was the guard. He saw a strong man in the dark, hollered, and ordered him to stop. Rostam stopped, laughed, and went to Giv on foot. Then, they both went to Kavus. Rostam told the king, "He is akin to Saam in stature. I do not know anyone like him among the heroes of Iran and Turan. Then, with no regard for the war, they celebrated until morning.

Sohrab's army stood against the Iranian army. Sohrab seized the higher ground with a view to the entire Iranian army, and asked his soldiers to bring him Hojir. He questioned him and asked him to tell the truth. Hojir pledged that he would tell the truth. Sohrab asked about the Iranian demons, and wanted to know about Rostam. Then, he showed Hojir all camps and flags one by one, and made him describe those heroes. Hojir said, "That seven-colored royal court and the leopard-patterned tents that represent the heart of the Iranian army with an image of the sun belong to Khosrow. Nowzar is to the left of the Tous army, with an elephant ensigned on its flag. The crimson royal court with the lion sign belongs to Goudarz.

The green court with a dragon on its flag belongs to an exemplary herculean hero in Iran whom I don't know, for he has just arrived from China." (Hojir was worried about introducing Rostam to Sohrab when he might have intended to kill Rostam. No one can avenge him.) He refrained from uttering Rostam's name. Sohrab, who was eager to hear Rostam's name from Hojir, and asked many questions about Rostam's green tent. Hojir dodged his questions and continued, "The flag with an image of a wolf belongs to Giv, the son of Goudarz and Rostam's son-in-law. There are many passages over there, and the commander sitting on the ebony throne is Fariborz, Kavus' son."

Sohrab kept asking about Rostam, and Hojir answered, "Rostam is on a hunt in Zabol, and has avoided war." Sohrab laughed and said, "Who would believe that when the King of Iran is at war, Rostam, the Hero of Iran, is on a hunt, making merry?" Hojir described Rostam's power and fighting abilities to put fear in his heart to persuade him against warring with him. He pondered, "I would rather die than let Iran fall." Sohrab struck his neck with the back of his hand, and Hojir fell down. He wore his armor, wielded his spear, mounted his steed, and went to the battlefield. No one from the Iranian army could dare look at him. He called Kavus disparagingly, and called on him to send his heroes to the battlefield. He attacked Kavus' court, and removed all the nails with a spear. The royal court of Kavus collapsed, and Kavus sent a messenger to Rostam.

"All other kings call me in times of celebration and war," said Rostam, "But Kavus always asks for me in times of war." He ordered his horse to be saddled. Heroes such as Giv, Gorgin, Roham, and Tous were preparing Rakhsh in fear of Sohrab. Rostam immediately put on his uniform and went to battle. He spotted Sohrab and told him, "This quarrel is between you and me, and we shall not involve the others. Whoever is killed will accept defeat and return to their country." "You are old," said Sohrab, "and couldn't withstand one punch from me." "I have seen many battles," replied Rostam, "and I have many heroes and demons; Wait and see me in battle." "I presume you are Rostam-e-Dastan." To his surprise, Rostam said, "I am not Rostam, for I have nothing." Sohrab was disappointed.

He was astounded by the signs his mother had told him, and his words. Rostam and Sohrab started fighting and launched spears at each other. The armor on their body was destroyed, but they perspired. They faced each other while one was afflicted from the separation of his son, and the other from the separation of his father. Rostam was aghast with his strength, for he had not struggled as much when fighting the White Demon. They both wielded bows, yet neither side was defeated. Finally, Rostam snatched Sohrab by the belt, but couldn't raise him from the saddle. Sohrab struck his shoulder with his mace, and Rostam twisted in pain but said nothing.

Furiously, Rostam attacked the army of Turan, and leaped at them like a wolf. Sohrab attacked the Iranian army, and killed many soldiers. Rostam was dispirited and said, "O blood-thirsty Turk, who will fight you from the army of Iran? Why do you attack sheep as a wolf?" "You attacked Turan first," said Sohrab, "and no one from the army came to fight you!" Rostam and Sohrab returned to their army to continue fighting the next day. Upon returning to his camp, Rostam assessed Sohrab's attack on the Iranian army. "Gorgin could not fight him and fled," said Giv. Rostam went to Kavus and expressed, "I have fought many battles, but I have never seen such a strong and brave warrior! Thus, I do not know who will prevail tomorrow." "I shall pray all night until dawn so that you may win," said Kavus. Rostam returned to his tent, asked for food from his brother, Zavareh, and talked to him, "Watch the army when I go to fight tomorrow. If I win, I shall return to you immediately. But if I am defeated and killed; do not fight him. Take the entire army back to Zabolestan to your father. Tell your parents not to mourn my fall, for it is of no use since no one stays on this earth forever. If Kavus seeks war, help him, and do not be indolent." Then, he slept. Sohrab returned to Hooman, and asked him to celebrate and rest from fighting.

On the next day, as Sohrab was putting on his armor, he told Hooman, "This hero has a stature similar to mine. hero has a stature similar to mine. When we clash, I hold no grudges against him. The signs are similar to how my mother described him. I think he is Rostam, for warriors like him are few and far between. Hooman intended to deceive Sohrab, saying, "I have clashed many times with Rostam. His horse is akin to Rakhsh but lacks its abilities."

 Sohrab was reassured and prepared to fight. He came to Rostam, asked how he was, and called on him to make peace and celebrate together instead of fighting. "O hero," said Rostam, "We have talked of wrestling; you cannot deceive me, for I am not a child. We shall fight and see what fate has in store for us." "I wished you would die in your bed instead of on the battlefield," said Sohrab, "But as you wish. If God wants your demise to be in my hand, be that as it may."

They brawled, and blood and sweat poured forth from their bodies. Sohrab raised him up and pounded him to the ground, then sat on his chest and tried to take his head off. Rostam said, "Us heroes do not kill those whose backs we put against the dirt, even if we have an enmity toward them." He deceived Sohrab to escape from his grasp. Sohrab listened, and stood up from his chest. He then left the battle on a hunt, and returned to the tent late. Hooman asked the reason, and Sohrab told him everything. "Are you giving up on life?!" said Hooman, "You let go of the lion you had caught so easily?" He angrily left Sohrab. After snatching release from Sohrab, Rostam went to a stream nearby. He washed himself up and prayed to God.

The third clash between Rostam and Sohrab commenced. When he saw him, Sohrab asked Rostam arrogantly how he was. They tussled again. Sohrab was trying to put Rostam on the ground with extreme force. Rostam realized this, and gathered all the strength he could muster and pounded him to the ground. He knew that Sohrab was a young man with strong arms, and would get up immediately. Thus, he removed his blade and pierced his side.

Sohrab twisted, sighed in pain, and told Rostam, "I have brought this evil upon myself, and you are innocent. Children of my age play in alleys, while I am dying on dirt. Know that wherever you go, my father, Rostam will come after you and avenge me. One of Iran's heroes will eventually tell Rostam, and you will pay the price."

Rostam was baffled and asked, "What do you know of Rostam? I am him." "If you are Rostam," said Sohrab, "Know that you have slain me in vain. I tried to make peace with you, and to tell you that you are my father, but you concealed your identity. As I was leaving the palace, my mother tied an orb to my arm to show to my father. My uncle accompanied me to introduce us, but Zhenderazm died, and you killed me. I have tied the orb to my arm. Have a look for yourself." Rostam untied his arm and saw it. He threw dirt on his head and wept blood. Sohrab consoled him and told him to stop crying.

There was no sign of Rostam for a long time. The Iranian army was anxious that he might have been killed. Kavus was told that Rostam had died. He ordered the entire Iranian army to assault the army of Turan. As the soldiers beat the drums of war and chaos, Sohrab asked his father to go to the king and stop the killing. Rostam jumped on Rakhsh and went to Kavus. The Iranians rejoiced to see him, and asked about the war. He told them everything. Iran's heroes, like Tous, Gostaham, and Goudarz went to Sohrab with him. Sohrab was taking his final breaths, and Rostam wanted to kill himself with his knife, but the elders prevented him.

Rostam asked Goudarz to go to Kavus to get panacea for Sohrab. Goudarz went to the king at once, and gave him the message. Kavus said, "If Sohrab recovers, father and son shall be united, and no one will be able to stop them. They will no longer obey me. Didn't you hear how Rostam belittled me? If he is the king of Iran, then who is Tous?" Goudarz returned to Rostam and said, "The king's waywardness is on display once again, and he doesn't give the panacea. You should go to him yourself and try to persuade him.

Rostam put Sohrab's head on a precious cloth, then mounted Rakhsh and went to Kavus. On his way, he was told that Sohrab had left the mortal world. He returned at once, went before his son, and wept. He then ordered a golden coffin to be built for him. All of Iran's heroes headed to Zabolestan with dirt on their heads and torn robes. Kavus said, "What of the war? How long will you cry?" "Hooman has returned his army to Turan," said Rostam, "And will not come here. Zavareh, my brother, will serve the King." "I am sorrowful of your loss," said the king, "Although I am not happy about Turan."

The king returned to the capital, and Rostam reached Zaal in Zabolestan, who opened his coffin in the palace and showed his body and face to his father. Zaal saw his resemblance to

Saam, and was shocked at how Rostam could fail to see that he was a descendant of Saam from how he wielded the mace. "I wish to make a golden tomb for him," said Rostam, "But I know that its gold will be plundered in war. Therefore, I shall make him a tomb out of horses' hooves." So he buried Sohrab as he wept blood.

# Siavash

Tous and Giv went on a hunt near the border with Turan. They saw a beautiful girl alone in the wilderness, approached her, and she said, "I am a descendant of Garsivaz and of Fereydoun's blood. My horse was exhausted and threw me down. Thieves attacked me and took my crown and jewelry. If my parents find out, they will surely send a rider after me." Giv and Tous both wanted the girl and quarreled over her. One of their associates asked them to go to Kavus and seek help. Upon seeing the girl, Kavus said, "This girl is of my blood, and should join my harem." Kavus married her.

The girl gave birth to a handsome boy, whom Kavus named Siavash. Astrologers observed the boy's fate to be turbulent. After some time, Rostam came to Kavus and asked him to nurture Siavash. Rostam took him to Zabol and trained him in riding, archery, and kings' manners. When Siavash was a grown-up, he wanted to see the king. Rostam packed provisions for travel and sent a large army with him. Siavash was informed of Kavus' arrival, and ordered Giv, Tous, and an army to welcome him. After seeing him, all attendants started to heap praise on him. Siavash bowed and sat next to the king, and Kavus thanked Rostam for his efforts. They held a ceremony, and were jolly for a week.

The king opened up his treasury and gave generously. He gave Kohistan (Mesopotamia) to Siavash, who was successful for eight years. At that time, Sudabeh (Siavash's wife) saw him and fell in love. She sent a messenger to bring him to her harem at night, but Siavash rejected her. Sudabeh went to the king the next night and asked Siavash to be taken to her sisters in her harem. The king agreed, and sent him away. Siavash thought that the king was testing him; and pondered, "If I go to the harem, Sudabeh will talk behind my back." Therefore, he asked the king to go to archery with the elders. The king insisted and sent him to see his sisters, and he finally agreed. The king sent a man named Herbad to look after him. Sudabeh and the women of the harem threw gems before his feet. Sudabeh had put on a crown and was sitting on the bed. When she saw Siavash, she immediately came down and bowed. Siavash went to his sisters, and immediately returned to his father. At night, the king went to Sudabeh's harem and sought Siavash. Sudabeh praised him, and asked the king to choose a spouse for him. The king called Siavash and said, "I wish for a king of kings from your lineage to succeed me." "Your wish is my command," said Siavash, "But I do not want someone from Sudabeh's harem."

The king assured Siavash that Sudabeh wanted what's best for him. Siavash bowed and left, but in his heart, he feared Sudabeh's duplicity. Sudabeh sent Herbad to bring Siavash. He put Siavash on the throne, sat next to him, and said, "From these idols, choose one." "I don't want to choose a wife from my enemies," contemplated Siavash, , "especially Sudabeh, who is the sly daughter of the king of Hamavaran." Sudabeh wanted to marry Siavash after the king's death, and got close to him. Siavash decided to calm her by flattering her, and said, "Your daughter is enough for me." He then left the harem, and Kavus came to the harem and saw Sudabeh. She told the king, "Siavash only loves my daughter." The king cheered up, and Sudabeh wondered, "If he disobeys me, I shall make life a living nightmare for him."

Sometime later, she sent someone after Siavash and said, "Let's enjoy our youthful virility. I love you, and my desire is to be with you. If you fail to heed my request, I shall make you fall out favor with the king." Siavash disagreed, and angrily arose to leave. Sudabeh grabbed him and said, "Do you wish to destroy my reputation?" She tore up her dress, clawed her face, and screamed. The king immediately went to the harem and asked what had happened. "Siavash fought me," said Sudabeh, "and said you are the only one I desire." The king pondered, "If she is telling the truth, I should part Siavash's head from his body." He took Siavash and Sudabeh to his chamber, and asked them to tell the truth. Siavash told him what had transpired. Sudabeh ejaculated, "I said nothing but the truth, and he is lying."

Kavus kissed Siavash's hand and body, and realized that he didn't smell of Sudabeh. So the king humiliated his spouse, sent her out, and told his associates, "We should make mincemeat of her." But the king feared the king of Hamavaran, for he was fond of him and his children were young.

When it dawned on Sudabeh that she had lost the king, she looked for a solution. A pregnant sorceress was her help. She made her servant promise to keep her secret, and gave her much gold and coins. At night, the sorceress had some medicine, aborted her two fetuses, and left the palace. Sudabeh sat on the bed, put the fetuses in a washtub, and screamed.

The palace of Kavus was shaken. The king woke up and asked the reason, and the nurses told him. Upon seeing Sudabeh and the two fetuses in the golden washtub, he was saddened. "See the truth," declared Sudabeh, "You showed Siavash mercy in vain." For a moment, Kavus became suspicious of Siavash. He called the sages to tell him the truth, but they couldn't observe anything. They said to the king, "If they weredescendants of the elites, their star would appear in the heavens." They told the king the mother's signs, and he kept it a secret from everyone but ordered his officers to find the sorceress. Sudabeh wept and begged the king for justice.

The sorceress was found in a week. He was brought to Kavus, but they couldn't force him to speak by kowtowing and threatened her with death. Out of fear, the sorceress revealed Sudabeh's secrets. A sage went to Sudabeh and recounted the sorceress' confessions. Sudabeh responded, "She is saying so in fear of Rostam, who is a supporter of Siavash. If you, too, are afraid to take my right from Siavash, I entrust him to God." She cried and so did the king, and he reflected, "I will get to the bottom of this."

The king called a mobad and asked his opinion, and he said, "You need to choose one and make them pass through the fire to reveal the liar." Sudabeh heard the news and said to the king, teary-eyed, "I have lost my two children, and I am now required to pass through the heart of fire. Make Siavash, who is the culprit behind this evil, walk through fire." Kavus was anxious, for if one of the two were guilty, how could he save the other? So he ordered to gather logs, and a fire was started. Siavash gladly agreed to walk through the fire.

Sudabeh watched the fire from the palace veranda, and wished for Siavash to burn in the fire. Siavash was wearing white and the scent of musk and camphor. The entire population gathered around the roaring fire, and Siavash braved into the fire on a horse. People looked for smoke, and saw him emerge from the fire unscathed. Sudabeh plucked her hair and clawed her face, but the king rejoiced. Siavash came to the king and bowed. Kavus embraced him, and thanked the Lord, and they celebrated for three days. On the fourth day, Kavus called Sudabeh and said, "For your slander against the king's son, you will be executed by hanging." "Siavash emerged from the fire unharmed due to Zaal's wizardry," she said, "I shall obey your command." The entire harem wept. Siavash came to Kavus and asked him to forgive Sudabeh. Kavus was waiting for the intercessor, and immediately forgave her.

After some time, Kavus was told that Afrasiab was marching toward Iran with hundred-thousand riders. The king assembled the elders, and discussed war with Afrasiab. Siavash was notified and told the king, "I shall go to war with Afrasiab." He wanted to be safe from Sudabeh's trickery and his father's suspicion. Kavus called Rostam, told him the story, and entrusted Siavash to him. "Siavash is my heart and soul," said Rostam, "And I shall protect him as if he was me." The king opened his treasury, and provided Siavash with twelve-thousand fighters. The king went to the army, lauded them, and wished them to be victorious. Kavus bid Siavash farewell, and returned. Siavash went to Zabol with his army. He was there for a month, then departed Kabul to Herat, and camped in Balkh. Garsivaz and Barman accompanied the army of Turan. They sent a messenger to Afrasiab, revealing the Iranian camp's position, "Rostam and Siavash are among the Iranian army."

The fighting continued for three days at the gate to Balkh. At last, Turan's army retreated back to Afrasiab's court. Siavash wrote a letter to Kavus informing him of the events, "My army has advanced until Jeyhun River. If you give the order, I shall cross the border and attack Turan." "Afrasiab is a sly Turk," said the king, "Keep your distance and do not disperse the army." Garsivaz bore the war news to Afrasiab, saying, "You are a fool to have started this war." Afrasiab was outraged, screamed at him, and kicked him out of his camp. Afrasiab went to sleep and jumped, screaming and fearful. Garsivaz came to him and said, "What are you hiding from your brother? Tell me your problem so we may resolve it." Afrasiab said, "I dreamed of a desert teeming with serpents and a sky with eagles. The earth was drought-stricken, and my army covered the horizons. Suddenly, dust collapsed my flag, and blood streamed from every corner. My entire army laid on the ground headless or wounded, and the Iranian army attacked my throne. They raised me up and took me to Kavus in shackles. The fourteen-year-old son of Kavus attacked me, and split me in half with his sword." "The dream is a bearer of good news," he responded, "It means your enemies will be destroyed, and you shall reach what you desire. However, we need to ask the sages and mobads to interpret your dream."

The mobads and sages were brought in, and he recounted his dream. They were given many coins so they would not fear interpreting his dream. A mobad asked for the king's blessing, and interpreted his dream thus, "A massive army commanded by a fortunate prince will come to fight us. If the king fights him, our country will be turned into ruin. If you slay him, your kingdom will be turned upside down, and the rebellions will start in the nation." Afrasiab was vexed and told Garsivaz, "We should not go to war with Siavash. Instead, we should promise him the crown and the throne, and make peace to keep disaster away." He then called the elders and consulted them.

He reminded them of his grandeur and luck, and told them of peace with Siavash. The king brought Garsivaz to Siavash and promised to give him the reign and the crown. "Tell Siavash," stated Afrasiab, "We are all descendants of Fereydoun. Turan and Iran are brothers, and I wish to bring peace to both nations. Iraj was slain innocently, and I do not want to repeat it. You are the prince of Iran. Talk with Kavus and Rostam, and keep war away from our lands." Garsivaz entered Balkh with many gifts, and Siavash and Rostam greeted him. Garsivaz discussed with them the king's suggestion. "Stay for a week and be merry," said Rostam, "And we shall respond." Siavash asked him to do research and ask why Afrasiab made the offer.

After a week, Siavash told Garsivaz, "If Afrasiab truly seeks peace, he should send the people wanted by Rostam, and leave the Iranian territories he is occupying. In this case, I shall secure the King of Iran's promise of peace with you." Garsivaz sent a messenger to Afrasiab. Instead, Afrasiab saw the name of a hundred of his associates, and was desolated. He immediately retreated from the cities of Bokhara, Sogda, Samarqand, Chach, and Sepichap all the way to Gang.

Garsivaz returned to Siavash and presented him with precious gifts. Rostam told Siavash, "Kavus is bitter. He will be enraged if he hears that we made peace with Turan. We should discuss the matter with him." He recounted the events of the war, and

Rostam took the letter to the king. Saam told Kavus the whole story. Kavus became irate and said, "Siavash is young and will fall for Afrasiab's trick. You have seen his slyness firsthand! Why did you trust him? Send a courier to Siavash and ask him to wreak havoc on the Turks, and bring me Afrasiab's associates so that I may take their heads." "We were ready for war," said Rostam, "He offered peace, and it is not becoming to start war. Now, we have what we wanted and took back our cities, and we should not dishonor our word." Kavus was angry and said, "You put this childish thought into his head. You did this for the sake of your own comfort. Stay here so that Tous may go to battle." "If Tous is more capable than me in warfare," said Rostam sadly, "From now on, ignore me."

He dashed out of Kavus' palace enraged. Kavus called the administrator, wrote a harsh letter to Siavash, and demanded that he start the war as soon as he arrived in Tous. The letter was delivered to Siavash. When Siavash came to know what had transpired between Rostam and Kavus, he said, "If I send the Turkish commanders to my father, he will hang them unduly, and I will be ashamed before God. If I fight Turan without reason, I will also be regretful before the Lord. If I return to my father, I will receive nothing from him and Sudabeh but evil." He called Bahram and Zangay to confide in them, "I came to war to escape Sudabeh. I took much treasure and recaptured our lost territories, but my father demands blood. I don't want to be subject to Kavus' wrath. Therefore, I shall go to a country away from the king's watch. Send the Turkish elders and Afrasiab's treasure to the king, and tell him everything."

He called Bahram, and gave him control of the army until Tous arrived to receive the treasure. Those two counseled Siavash to persuade his father or obey the king himself, but Siavash was not convinced. Thus, the two downhearted heroes announced their loyalty. Then, Zangay went to Afrasiab and delivered Siavash's message. Afrasiab was agitated, and consulted with Piran, who said, "Siavash is an exceptional and renowned prince. If you accept him and arrange a marriage between him and your daughter, the enmity between Iran and Turan will be gone. After all, Kavus is old and not long for this world, and Siavash will succeed him. Thus, you will secure your future, and that of your descendants."

Afrasiab penned a letter to Siavash, "If you come to me, I shall love you as a son; and the entirety of Turan will obey you. I shall entrust my throne to you, and whenever you decide to make peace with your father, I shall send you off to Iran with the crown and the golden belt." Siavash read Afrasiab's letter and wrote to his father, "You made me walk through fire for a woman's trickery. Your harem became my prison. If you have had enough of me, I shall put myself in the fangs of dragons with the fate that it entails." Then, he told Bahram what was necessary, and went to Afrasiab with 300,000 warriors. The elders and the army were waiting by the water. They bowed before Siavash. Piran kissed him, and thanked the Lord for reaching there in health.

They reached the city of Gang and Afrasiab greeted him on foot. He embraced him and they complimented each other; they went to Afrasiab›s palace, and celebrated for a week. Years passed. One day, Afrasiab asked Siavash to play a game of polo. Siavash struck the orb strongly and it vanished. Then, Afrasiab asked him to put an arrow on the mark. Siavash was right on target, and the second arrow split the first. All the elders congratulated him. After these two tests, Afrasiab and Siavash were friends in sorrow and joy; and he no longer confided in Garsivaz and Jahn (one of Turan's elders). One year passed. Piran asked Siavash to marry his daughter, Jarirah. Siavash accepted, and there was a marriage ceremony.

Over the years, Siavash became more and more dear to Afrasiab, but he had enemies in the court who were eager to destroy him. One day, Piran addressed Siavash, "To strengthen your power, you should marry Farangis, Afrasiab's daughter." He went to Afrasiab and proposed to Farangis, saying, "The sages have said that a descendant of Afrasiab and Kavus will become a mighty king." He persuaded Afrasiab, and returned to Siavash. Piran arranged the marriage and sent Farangis valuable gifts. They celebrated and danced for one week. Then, Afrasiab bestowed China and Khotan to Siavash; and Siavash and Piran traveled to Khotan.

After some time, Siavash longed for Iran, confided in Piran, and stated that a terrible death awaited him in Turan. Piran became somber and wondered, "If it is so, I am at fault for dragging you to this land." They made merry for seven days, and on the eighth day, a letter from the king commanded them to go to the sea of Sindh and collect taxes from those nations. Siavash assembled his army and set off. On the way, he received another letter from Afrasiab stating, "I have not seen joy since you left. If you are happy there, stay; otherwise, return to me." Siavash traveled to the surrounding nations and collected their taxes, then built a paradisaical city called Siavashgard. Piran came from India and China to see the city, and Siavash welcomed him. He then congratulated Siavash.

Piran met Farangis, whereupon he returned to Afrasiab, told him the whole story, described the beauty of Siavashgard, and gave him the collected taxes. Afrasiab rejoiced that his daughter was happy. He told the story to Garsivaz, and asked him to go to Siavash with precious gifts. Garsivaz went to Siavash with an army, and was greeted warmly. They brought news that Jarirah had given birth to a son resembling Siavash. Siavash named him Frood, and Garsivaz went to Farangis and complained of the king's selfishness and the rule of Siavash. He was upset about Siavash's progress and envied him. Therefore, he arranged several races, but Siavash defeated the Turks in all competitions. Then, he asked Siavash to fight him one on one, but Siavash kept refusing. At last, Siavash agreed to fight Gorvi and Damor.

First, Siavash raised Gorvi and Damor from their saddles and threw them over. They stayed with Siavash for a week, and returned to the capital on the eighth day. Afrasiab was happy to hear the news and laughed, and Garsivaz was green with envy. One night, he went to Afrasiab's harem, and told him that Siavash had a messenger from Kavus: That has conspired with Rome and China, assembled a massive army, and intended to destroy Turan.

Afrasiab was ill at ease and reflected for three days. Then, he told Garsivaz, "Siavash left the throne and took refuge in me. He has not disobeyed me to this day. I entrusted my daughter to him, and he looks after her. I have nothing to make me suspicious of him. If I do wrong by Siavash, I will become infamous. The only way is to go after his father, in which case our nation will be reduced to ruins." Garsivaz would use any tricks he would come up with to make the king skeptical of Siavash.

One day, the king called Garsivaz and said, "Go to Siavash and tell him that my heart longs for him, and ask him to come to me with Farangis. I need to meet you." Garsivaz went to the king and delivered Afrasiab's message. Siavash was elated. Garsivaz deviously started to weep. Siavash was sorrowful of his sadness, and asked the reason. "They have spread lies about you to Afrasiab and changed his view of you for the worst." "Fear not," said Siavash, "The Lord is with me and protects me. Afrasiab favors me as his son and has raised me to greatness. I will come to the capital with you and ask the reason."

Garsivaz spoke of Afrasiab's wickedness and how he slew his own brother, Agrirath the Wise. He then said, "Stay here. I will write a letter of apology to the king and go to him myself to earn his support. Send letters to the heads of China and Iran and ask them for an army. If Afrasiab softens his stance, I will send you a messenger to come to him, and if he insists on vengeance, fight him with your army." Siavash wrote a letter to Afrasiab, and made Farangis' illness the excuse for refusing to go. He gave the letter to Garsivaz, who galloped for three days restlessly, and reached Afrasiab's palace on the fourth. He talked at length of Siavash's pride, "He has assembled a massive army, and if you stall, he will take Turan." Afrasiab was furious and departed with his army.

On the other side, Siavash went to Farangis shaking, and said, "My end in Turan is nigh." Farangis wept, "What are you doing? Neither Iran, Rome, nor China is safe for you. You can only seek shelter in God." Siavash screamed and woke up on the fourth night, and Farangis asked him why. He said, "I saw a river flush with water and a mountain of fire, and lancers lined up on both sides, end to end. There was a fire on one side and water on the other, and against me stood Afrasiab and his army. Garsivaz had kindled the fire, and I was burning in it." Thereafter, Siavash assembled his army, and Afrasiab and his army lined up against him. Garsivaz came to Siavash and said, "My advice was fruitless. You need to prepare your army for battle." Farangis said, "O my King of Kings, leave Turan." "I sense my death is near," declared Siavash, "You have been pregnant for five months. If I had a son, name him Kay Khosrow, and dedicate your whole life to him. I know that they will cut off my head without guilt and no tomb or shroud will be left of me."

He bid Farangis farewell and went to the stall. He put his horse Shabrang, and whispered in its ear, "Do not yield to anyone until my son Kay Khosrow comes for my vengeance. Then, allow him to ride you." He released the other horses, then walked for half a parasang and reached Afrasiab's army. They looked at each other, and none had any enmity toward the other. Garsivaz said, "If you are innocent, why have you come before the king in armor?" Siavash realized that that fool had forced the king to do this. Afrasiab declared war. The Iranians prepared for war, but Siavash did not let them, and surrendered.

Gorvi tied his hands and dragged him along to Siavashgard. The king ordered him to cut off his head and pour his blood on the dirt. Piran's brother, Pilsam, told Afrasiab, "Do not hasten, for you will regret this. Piran will arrive tomorrow. Wait and hear his arguments." Garsivaz foolishly said, "Your highness, if you hesitate, the Roman and Chinese army will come to his help. If you forgive him, I will not stay with you." Damor and Gorvi supported him. "I do not consider him guilty," said Afrasiab, "But what shall I do for this is what fate has written for him." Farangis came to her father weeping, and begged him to forgive Siavash. By the king's order, she was put under house arrest. Then, he ordered Siavash to be taken somewhere remote, cut his head off, and pour his blood on the dry desert.

Gorvi took him to a desert, butchered his head in a golden washtub, and released his blood into the desert. The curse of a nation was upon Gorvi. After Siavash's killing, Farangis cut off her hair and cursed Afrasiab. Her cries and curses reached Afrasiab, and he told Garsivaz, "Bring her to the street. Pull her hair, and beat her with sticks until she miscarries. I don't want a child to be born out of Siavash's seed." Pilsam, Lahhak, and Farshidvard went to Piran and told him everything. Piran fell down from his seat and lost consciousness. Pilsam woke him up and said, "Hurry before they kill Farangis also."

They galloped their horses to the city, and found Farangis unconscious and surrounded by swordsmen on horses. Piran the guards to talk to Afrasiab. He immediately went to the king and said, "I know you will live to regret this. Why are you killing your own daughter?! She is bearing a child. If you kill her, the people will curse you for eternity. Send her to my palace. I shall look after her until she gives birth; then, I'll kill her." Afrasiab agreed. Piran took her to his palace and looked after her until labor.

# Kay Khosrow's Birth

One night, Piran dreamed of Siavash, who said loudly, "Arise! Kay Khosrow has been born." When he woke up, Golshahr (his wife) took him to Farangis. Piran saw a child deserving of the throne. He immediately went to Afrasiab and told him that the child is very similar to Tur and Fereydoun. He advised Afrasiab, made him regret Siavash's death, and decided to let the child live. Afrasiab told Piran, "Send him to shepherds on the mountain, for they won't know his lineage." Piran did as the king commanded.

Seven years passed. Kay Khosrow was always on a hunt, and when he turned ten, the Shepherd came to Piran and said, "He is constantly on a hunt, and I fear that he may harm himself." Piran went to the mountain, and embraced Kay Khosrow. Kay Khosrow was surprised and asked, "Why are you embracing a child shepherd?" Piran was distraught and said, "You are a prince, not a shepherd's son." He then took him back to his palace. When he was asleep, a messenger from Afrasiab came to Piran and said, "The king is anxious about Siavash's son. If he decides to avenge his father, we should cut off his head." Piran went to Kay Khosrow and said, "I will take you before the king. Conceal your wisdom and reason, and speak of celebration and joy no matter what he asks."

Piran dressed him up as a prince and took him to the palace. Afrasiab trembled when he saw Kay Khosrow. He then asked question, and Kay Khosrow gave nonsensical answers. Afrasiab was relieved, and ordered Piran to take him and his mother to Siavashgard and provide them with everything they needed. The people of Siavashgard received them warmly, and rejoiced to see them. In the desert, a tree had grown from Siavash's blood.

Some time passed. The spies informed Kavus of Siavash's death. He tore apart his robes and poured dirt on his head. The entire nation of Iran mourned for him. When news reached Sistan, Rostam passed out and mourned for a week. On the eighth day, he assembled a massive army from Kashmir and Kabul, went to Kavus, and said, "Your malicious ways meant Siavash's death. You chose the love of sly Sudabeh, and killed the future king of kings." Kavus looked at his sorrowful face and said nothing. Rostam went to Sudabeh's harem, pulled her hair, dragged her to Kavus, and split her in two with the sword. Kavus didn't even twitch. All the heroes of Iran gathered, and Rostam announced, "I swear by Yazata that I will avenge Siavash, and I will butcher that coward, Gorvi, like a lamb." Everyone screamed, and Iran was filled with hate for Afrasiab. Rostam chose twelve-thousand warriors for Faramarz, and asked him to go the king of Sepichab near the border with Turan. He sent along thirty-thousand swordsmen. Faramarz went to him and asked about Afrasiab; but the king of Sepichab did not help him, and the two armies fought. At last, Faramarz decapitated Varazaad, the king.

Afrasiab heard this and rued his past deeds. He sent Sarkheh, his son, to fight Faramarz. Faramarz and Sarkheh clashed, and Faramarz put his spear in him. The army of Turan came to aid Sarkheh, and he managed to escape. Faramarz and the Iranian army chased them. At last, Faramarz raised Sarkheh from the saddle, pounded him to the ground, and dragged him to his camp. Rostam and his army arrived, and found the desert filled with dead bodies. Rostam ordered Sarkheh to be taken to the desert, and have his head chopped off as they had done to Siavash. Tous volunteered for this task. "Why do you wish to spill my blood when I'm innocent?" asked Sarkheh, Siavash was my friend and brother, and I am tormented by his death." Tous felt sorry for him, and told Rostam. "Afrasiab should be forever sorrowful and weeping," said Rostam. Then, Zavareh volunteered to kill Sarkheh. He took Sarkheh to the desert, cut off his head, and crucified his body.

The news was delivered to Afrasiab. He tore up his clothes, and poured dirt on his own head. He assembled an army and went to war with Iran. Pilsalm asked him to go fight Rostam. Afrasiab said, "Bring me Rostam's head, and I'll marry you to my daughter and give you the reigns." Piran was upset and tried to stop him from fighting. He did, however, enter the arena and call Rostam. Giv went to fight him, but could not defeat him and was joined by Faramarz. Still, they couldn't defeat Pilsam. Rostam left and called him. Pilsalm approached him, and Rostam put his spear into his hip, raised him from the saddle, took him toward the army of Turan, and threw him over. Pilsalm died, and the two armies attacked each other. The ensuing dust cloud made the two armies invisible to each other. Afrasiab called the army to attack the Iranians from all sides. Rostam, Faramarz, and Tous attacked Turan's shield-bearers and killed many. Rostam and Afrasiab brawled, but Afrasiab's strikes were ineffectual. Rostam hit Afrasiab's horse and knocked him over; then tried to kill him, but Hooman struck the mace on his shoulder, and before Rostam could turn around, Afrasiab fled.

Rostam chased after Hooman on horseback but couldn't find him. Then, the army of Turan fled the Iranians. Rostam pursued them for three parasangs, and then returned to their camp. The next day, Rostam attacked Turan. Afrasiab ordered Siavash's son and Farangis to be taken to prevent Rostam from taking them to Iran and seating him on the throne. Rostam's army killed people and plundered Turan for six years. At last, he was informed that Kavus had become old and frail, and Afrasiab could attack and conquer Iran. Therefore, Rostam went to Zabol, and Tous, Goudarz, and Giv returned to the capital. When Afrasiab heard that Rostam had returned, he was elated. He found his nation burnt and ruined; and a drought engulfed Iran for seven years.

One night, he dreamed of Goudarz and a rain cloud covered the sky. A voice said, "If you want to receive the Lord's rain of mercy, bring king Kay Khosrow, son of Siavash, to Iran, your land shall flourish, and he may avenge his father. No one but Giv should follow him. Goudarz woke up, thanked God, called Giv at once, and described his dream. At dawn, Giv departed to Turan. While bidding farewell, he asked his father to look after Bijan's son. Giv passed through Turan's border alone and spoke Turkish along the way so that no one would recognize him. He asked for clues about Kay Khosrow. He chose a travel guide, and made him promise to tell truths to return whatever wealth he desired. Next, he asked about Kay Khosrow. The guide said that he had yet to hear such a name; and Giv immediately unsheathed his sword and put him down.

For seven years, Giv searched Turan for Kay Khosrow. One day, he reached a meadow, angered by the fruitlessness of his endeavors, stopped his horse, and lied down. He plotted to find Khosrow, and pondered, "Perhaps Kay Khosrow is not yet born?" Next to a faraway spring, he saw a tall young man drinking. He was akin to Manuchehr and king-like. Giv felt attached to him, and rushed to his side. Kay Khosrow saw him and wondered, "This must be Giv." Giv bowed before him and said, "I suppose you are the son of Siavash." Kay Khosrow answered, "And I presume you are Giv, son of Goudarz, the hero of Iran. My mother has talked extensively about you." Then, he told Giv all the disasters that had befallen him.

Giv saw Siavash's sign in Khosrow's body, and was put at ease. He then hugged him and asked about Kavus and his old age. After that, they both headed to Siavashgard. Kay Khosrow talked to Farangis, and the three agreed to move to Iran. Before their departure, Farangis asked Kay Khosrow to go to the meadow near the spring at dawn, and take Siavash's horse, taken for a drink by Behzad. Kay Khosrow went to the spring. Behzad was elated to see him, and talked extensively about Siavash. Then, he put the saddle on Shabrang, and gave it to him. Farangis opened up her hidden treasury, and they took as much as they could carry and journeyed to Iran.

Piran heard that they were on their way. He chose three-hundred riders to bring him the heads of Giv and Farangis, and to deliver Kay Khosrow in ropes. Giv saw the army from afar, attacked them, and killed many. The heroes escaped to Piran and told him the story. Piran chose a thousand warriors to stop Kay Khosrow from reaching Iran. They looked for Giv and Kay Khosrow day and night, to no avail. Finally, Farangis and company reached a river. Giv and Khosrow slept from exhaustion, but Farangis couldn't. He spotted the flag of Turan from afar, and immediately called Giv. Giv said, "You and Kay Khosrow climb the mountain, and with God's grace, I shall prevail." Kay Khosrow was eager to fight Turan, but Giv stopped him and said, "I have seventy-eight brothers. If I die, someone will replace me; whereas only you deserve Iran's throne, and if you are harmed; seven years of my efforts would be wasted."

Piran saw Giv and cussed at him. Giv raised Piran from the saddle with his lasso, threw him on the ground, and dragged him up the river. He then tied his hands and snapped his flag. The army of Turan attacked him. Like a roaring lion, Giv blitzed them and slew many soldiers of Turan. The River Hamoon was filled with the dead, and Turan's massive army fled. Giv returned to Piran and decided to decapitate him.

Piran bowed before Kay Khosrow and said, "The king knows my struggle and the reason for my perseverance in fighting." Farangis also wept and said, "He saved us from death." "But I have taken an oath to kill him when I see him," declared Giv. Kay Khosrow answered, "Pierce his ear so that blood may drip from your dagger, and remain faithful to your vow."

Then, Giv tied his hands hard such that no one, except his wife Golshahr, could open them. Then, he pierced his ears, put him on a horse, and sent him to Turan.

Afrasiab was informed of the event. He was saddened and said, "The army was exhausted and retreated while fighting one man!" Piran appeared with his army, and his head and neck were bloody. As they approached the king, he saw that Piran was riding the horse with his hands tied and his ear pierced. They tried yet failed to untie him. Piran told them the entire story. Afrasiab bellowed and cursed. He ordered his army to go to River Jeyhun and put them down.

On the other side, Kay Khosrow and Giv reached River Jeyhun and needed a vessel to cross it. The ship captain asked them to give him four things his heart desired: The first, Siavash's armor, gifted to Giv by Farangis; the second, Farangis, an enchanting young woman; the third, Siavash's horse, which Kay Khosrow was riding, and the fourth, Kay Khosrow. Giv was ready to give him the taxes of one city, but he refused. Then, Giv turned to Kay Khosrow, "We don't have much time. We should get into the water and cross the river on our horses." "If you are Kay Khosrow," said the captain, "You can cross Jeyhun, as Fereydoun did before he spread justice worldwide."

Kay Khosrow prayed the God. All three entered the water and crossed it safely. Kay Khosrow thanked God. The captain swallowed his tongue and took the ship to leave. Afrasiab and his army arrived, but Kay Khosrow was nowhere to be seen. Afrasiab asked the captain, and he complimented Kay Khosrow until he ran out of breath. Finally, Afrasiab asked the captain to board the ship and take them to the river. "O king of kings," said Hooman, "You will be entering Iran, and we will have to face Rostam."

Henceforth, Afrasiab and his army returned; and Kay Khosrow and Giv entered Iran. Giv wrote a letter to the heroes and the king, informing them of Kay Khosrow's arrival. First, he sent a messenger to Goudarz in Isfahan. When Giv's letter reached Kavus, the cries of joy echoed inside the palace. The entire country was decorated with ornaments, and people all around Iran celebrated and danced. The elders and heroes went to Isfahan, and so did Kay Khosrow and Giv. Goudarz seated him on the golden throne, and bestowed upon him gold and coins. He wept profusely over Siavash.

They celebrated for one week, and then departed for Kavus. Kavus embraced him, and kissed his head and eyes. Kay Khosrow recounted all the events to elderly Kavus, including Afrasiab's test, where he pretended to be stupid until Giv's fighting and rescue. Then, they entered the king's veranda.

Tous was so upset about Kay Khosrow's arrival that he sent an insulting message. Giv said, "Do not be fooled by Ahriman, and do not ruin our times of joy." "I am Manuchehr's grandson," said Tous, "and a renowned hero after Rostam. You cast a vote without my knowledge and chose a king. You chose someone of Afrasiab's blood to be the king of Iran. Fariborz, the son of Kavus, is more deserving of the throne."

Giv came to Goudarz, and discussed Tous' complaint. Goudarz assembled an army, and faced off Tous. Tous pondered, "If we fight today, many will be slain on both sides, and only Afrasiab will cheer." Then, he sent a messenger to Kavus. The king asked them to his palace. Tous said, "The king's son is the most competent custodian of the throne." Goudarz gave him many advises, then told Kavus, "Ask for both, and test them to see who is more deserving." "I ask them to go to the city of Ardabil in separate groups," said Kavus, "Demons dwell in Bahman Dezh, and won't let people in. Whoever destroys them while wielding a blade shall succeed me." Goudarz and Tous both liked this approach.

At dawn, Fariborz and Tous went to Kavus. Tous said, "I shall send the army and the elephants with Fariborz, and we shall vanquish Ahriman." So they headed to Bahman Dezh with an army. When they arrived, they found tall walls that no one could climb over. It was so hot that the armored soldiers burned. They kept looking but couldn›t find a way into the fortress.

After one week, they couldn't find anything and returned hopelessly.

Then, Goudarz assembled his army and went to Bahman Dezh with Kay Khosrow. He called his secretary and wrote a letter filled with praise of the Lord. In his letter, he wrote, "If this fort is the land of demons who are enemies of the Lord, I shall cleanse it with God's command and my mace. If sorcery is involved, I shall put them in shackles; and if God rules this fort, I shall return to it." He tied the letter to the spear's tip and hoisted it as if it were a flag. Giv placed the letter on the fort's wall and uttered the Lord's name. The letter disappeared immediately, and the wall cracked. Kay Khosrow ordered arrows to be launched inside at once. A cloud covered the sky, and there was a hailstorm. Many demons were vanquished.

Then, the sky cleared, and the gate to the fort became visible. The demons became obedient to the king. Kay Khosrow entered the fortress and saw a beautiful city with gardens, a palace, and a veranda. Kay Khosrow ordered to build a place with towering arches, and named it Azargoshasp. Then, he put mobads, sages, and scientists in the fire temple. Finally, he returned to Kavus in a year. News of his victory reached the king, and all heroes, including Fariborz and Tous, came to greet him. Kavus put Kay Khosrow on the throne, and placed the king's crown on his head.

# Kay Khosrow

Kay Khosrow put the crown on his head, and wherever he saw ruins, he rebuilt them and helped the needy. The elders of all nations came to him. At last, news reached Sistan that Khosrow had come from Turan to Iran. Rostam, along with Zaal, Zavareh, Faramarz, and all the elders of Sistan, went to the capital to kiss his ring. Khosrow was elated, for he knew that he had raised his father, Siavash. Giv, Goudarz, and Tous went to welcome him. Rostam asked about his condition, and tears streamed from his eyes. They talked until midnight about their past. At dawn, the king's drumbeats started, and elders such as Tous, Goudarz, Gorgin, Gostaham, and Bahram accompanied Rostam to a hunting ground. After that, they reached prosperous areas; and Khosrow gave generously wherever he went. Finally, they reached Azerbaijan, went to the Azargoshasp fire temple, and prayed to God. Then, they went to Kavus, and celebrated with Rostam and Zaal.

Khosrow told them what Afrasiab had done to him. Kavus asked him to avenge the blood of Siavash from Turan. Khosrow wrote an oath and gave it to Rostam, and they celebrated for one week. On the eighth day, they prayed to God. Kay Khosrow told Rostam, "You know that Afrasiab is very rude and shameless. He knows how to destroy, and has spilled the blood of innocent Siavash. Join me in avenging my father's blood." Rostam agreed. He headed to Kavus' throne, asked the heroes for assistance, and said, "Lend me a hand in avenging my father's blood. Know that Afrasiab started this enmity, and should pay for what he has done." They all vowed to help him on his journey.

Then, he ordered them to write the names of the elders and heroes in a notebook, and invited them to Khosrow. The king gifted them with plenty of treasure. Then, they brought precious gifts, and Khosrow told the heroes, "These gifts are for the one who brings me the head of Palashan, one of Afrasiab's heroes." Bijan, the son of Giv the Brave, stood up and volunteered. They brought other gifts by the king's order, and he said, "I shall give these to the one who brings me Tageuo's crown." Bijan stood up once again and announced his readiness. Several gifts and beautiful maids were brought, and the king announced, "I want a beautiful woman named Espino." Bijan stood up again. Khosrow was joyous, ordered many precious gifts to be brought, and announced, "These gifts are for the one who brings me Tageuo's head." This time, Giv volunteered. More gifts were brought, and the king asked for someone to go and sack Kasehrud. Giv volunteered again.

Once again, more precious gifts and several maids were brought, and the king said, "These belong to the person who delivers my message to Afrasiab and returns with his response." This time, Gorgin, son of Milad, stood. Then, they celebrated and cheered. Rostam and Faramarz accompanied them. Rostam spoke of a beautiful city filled with treasure and elephants built by Manuchehr in Zabolestan. "When Kavus became old," said Rostam, "Turan took the city, and they are receiving royalties and harassing the people. Therefore, we should send an army to drive Turan away. Khosrow said, "Give Faramarz the army he needs for this task."

They assembled a massive army, and heroes such as Fariborz, Goudarz, Roham, Giv, Shidush, and Bijan accompanied him. Khosrow approached an elephant, and witnessed a sea of soldiers. His heart became warm, and he advised Faramarz, "You are the son of Rostam, and Qanuj to Sistan belongs to you. Do not attack the defenseless. Help the desperate and the people. Know your friend and your enemy. Do not grow fond of the world, for our time will one day end. May God be pleased with you." Faramarz kissed the ground and went forth. Rostam went with him for some time, counseled him, and then returned. Faramarz climbed the horse, and went with the army.

# Akvan Div

One day, Kay Khosrow held a ceremony starting at dawn. The elders, including Goudarz, Rostam, Gostaham, Garshasp, Giv, Roham, Gorgin, and Kharad were also present. An hour passed by. The king's shepherd came and said, "I saw a zebra in the color of the sun in the herd, which was as ferocious as a lion. The zebra attacked the horses, and tore them apart." Khosrow realized that it was not a zebra, and told Rostam, "Go with haste, and kill that demon." Rostam obliged, and went to the wilderness. He looked for the demon for three days. On the fourth day, he saw a zebra passing by him at speed, and pursued it on Rakhsh. He then wondered, "I should catch this animal with a lasso, and take it to the king alive." The zebra disappeared from his view. Rostam realized that it was not the time for swordplay and he needed to use deception. He reflected, "I've heard from wise men that Akvan Div hides here and wears zebra skin." The demon appeared again, and the commander raced his horse. He prepared his lasso, and launched an arrow toward it. The demon disappeared again.

The demon wandered the wilderness for three days and three nights. Thirsty and sleepy, he found a spring, stepped off his horse, drank water, quenched Rakhsh's thirst, and slept. The demon saw him sleeping and came near. Akvan Div said, "Tell me whereupon the earth would you like me to drop you?" Rostam pondered, "If it drops me on a mountain, all my bones will be crushed. It's better if it drops me into the sea so that the fish eat me. But if I say drop me in the ocean, it will drop me toward a mountain." "Throw me on a mountain so that tigers and lions see me," asked Rostam.

Akvan immediately launched him toward the sea to be eaten by fish. Immediately after reaching the sea, Rostam reached for his dagger and killed the whales that tried to kill him. He then swam, reached dry land, and thanked the Lord for his salvation. Then, he put his lasso and weapon aside to let them dry. He returned to the spring where he had slept, but Rakhsh was nowhere to be found; so he looked around on foot. Finally, he saw Rakhsh among king Afrasiab's mares, and saddled it up. The shepherd woke up from the ruckus and woke up the guard to arrest the thief. Rostam introduced himself, and killed two groups among them. Afrasiab and his companions there could not find the shepherd and the horses. The shepherd came to the king and told him the story, and Afrasiab ordered all to look for Rostam.

When he saw them, he rained arrows on their heads, and killed some more with his mace. Then, he took all their things and returned to the spring to face Akvan again. This time, he smashed his sledge on the demon's head and killed it. He swiftly cut off its head and thanked God. Then, Rostam took the demon's head, took the Turks' war spoils, and headed to

Khosrow's court. The heroes greeted him and went to the king. Rostam kissed the ground; and by the king's order, distributed the spoils of war and the horses among the Iranians. They celebrated for one week, and Rostam told the story of Akvan Div to the king. Khosrow was astounded by his strength, and congratulated him. After two weeks, Rostam decided to go to Zaal. The king gifted him precious presents, and sent him to Sistan.

## Bijan and Manijeh

One day during a feast and a celebration with Iran's heroes, vengeance for Siavash's blood was rekindled in Kay Khosrow. A group of Armenians living in the city of Armanian on the border of Iran and Turan came to seek justice in the palace, and the guard took them to the king. They bowed before the king, weeping, and said, "We have come from the city of Arman to seek justice. Every once in a while, Turan's soldiers attack the city and lay waste to us; and recently, wild boars have started to attack our forests and fields and destroy our farms. There are too many of them, and they tear apart our animals with their fangs. O just king, we expect assistance from you."

The king was troubled and turned to the heroes, "O elders of Iran, which among you is ready to fight the boars? Whoever goes to fight will receive many gifts from me." None of the heroes spoke, except Bijan, the son of Giv, who stood up and volunteered. Giv was troubled and tried to stop him; but Bijan had made up his mind. So the king rejoiced and asked Gorgin to accompany him and show him the way.

Together, they headed to Armenia and hunted anything that crossed their path. When they reached Armanian, Bijan saw the wild boars. He asked Gorgin to go near the pond, push the boars to his side, and then hit them with arrows. "This was not the plan," complained Gorgin, "You volunteered to fight them."

Bijan was agitated but went into the field like a lion and fired arrows at the boars. Unfortunately, a boar attacked him and destroyed his armor. Bijan killed the beast with a dagger, and pulled its teeth to take it to the king.

Gorgin was taken aback by his bravery, but pretended to encourage him. Then, he tried to set a trap for him and said, "There is a lush green hill near the border with Turan, and this season, Afrasiab›s enchanting daughter, Manijeh, has come there for a stroll. If you agree, we will go there, choose some beautiful maids for the king, and take them to the palace." Bijan agreed and they went there. Bijan told Gorgin, "I'll lead to see that place." So he put on a stylish dress, went to the grove, and stood under a tree.

Manijeh saw him as she was looking around from inside her tent. He resembled Siavash, and she fell in love at first sight. She then sent along her kind nurse to ask him, "Are you Siavash, who has come back to life, or someone else?" The nurse departed and relayed Manijeh›s message.

"I am not Siavash," he answered, "I'm Bijan, son of Giv, and I've come here to kill boars. I killed them and pulled their teeth for the king. They told me of your festivity, and I came here to see Afrasiab's daughter, Manijeh." The nurse returned to the girl. By Manijeh's order, the nurse brought Bijan to the tent. They talked and dined for a while.

They stayed there for three days and three nights, and it was time for Bijan to leave. Manijeh ordered to lace his drink with sleeping drugs, and took him to Manijeh's palace. When Bijan woke up, he found himself in Afrasiab's veranda and said, "Gorgin will come for me and will reduce this palace atop Afrasiab's head." Manijeh asked him to be happy instead of angry, and held a feast. They celebrated and cheered in Afrasiab's palace for a few days. After some time, the guard was made aware and wanted to know who Bijan was. When he recognized him, he was terrified and went to Afrasiab. The king shivered like a leaf and consulted his elders. Eventually, he decided to send Garsivaz to Manijeh to bring Bijan in chain. Garsivaz entered the palace, and heard melodies and music. He ordered his soldiers to block all roads, and entered the palace. He spotted Bijan, and his eyes became red with blood. Bijan was not wearing his armor, and did not know how to fight him. He reached for the blade he always kept in his boot, stood before Garsivaz, and threatened him. Garsivaz knew that Bijan was truly capable of anything, so he didn't approach him. Then, he started making promises until he took the blade from him.

He then tied him up, and took him to Afrasiab undressed. Bijan told the king of Turan the whole story, and said that Manijeh had put him into sleep and taken him to his palace. Afrasiab didn't buy it, and said, "You came to fight the boars naked?!" "If you don't believe me, give me a horse and a mace," said Bijan, "And send along a thousand elders with me to battle, and survey the chaos I can cause while naked!" Afrasiab trembled in fear, and ordered Garsivaz to execute him by hanging him with his hands tied. Bijan was troubled, for he was about to be executed like cowards and sinners, and pondered, "The heroes of Iran will admonish me in death, and I will be ashamed before my father."

  As the soldiers were preparing the gallows, Piran came. First, he ordered to stop the execution and talk to the king. Then, he went to the king and said, "You killed Siavash and know what a grave mistake it was. If you kill Bijan also, the Iranians will try to avenge Siavash's blood, and Rostam will once again slaughter Turan's heroes." "He was with my daughter," said Afrasiab, "After this, my entire harem will ridicule me. This embarrassment will haunt me forever, and the people and the army will laugh at me."

Piran asked to put him in shackles instead of into death as a lesson to Iranian. Then, they put him in shackles, threw him into a well, and an elephant dragged the stone of Akvan Div over the well. He ordered Manijeh to be taken nearby to hear his cries and see his death. Manijeh would scavenge bread and drop it for Bijan through a hole to sustain him.

On the other side, Gorgin had been waiting for a week and had not heard of Bijan. Gorgin became sorrowful and looked for him, and saw Bijan's horse without a saddle, and realized that something terrible had happened to him. He immediately returned to Iran, informed Giv of Bijan's death, and entrusted his horse to him. Giv fell down from the horse and passed out. When he woke up, he reprimanded Gorgin, and he told him the story, "We went to fight the boars, killed them, pulled their death, and were on our way back to the king. We saw a hulking zebra and Bijan threw a lasso to catch it. The zebra took him and I lost sight of him. I roamed the mountain and the desert, but couldn't find him." Giv knew that he was lying and that his son was alive. He went to Kay Khosrow and complained of Gorgin.

Kay Khosrow heard the story and said, "I do not believe that Bijan is dead. Do not worry. I shall send my army after him. If they have killed him, I shall reduce Turan to dust, and avenge him and Siavash." Then, he called Gorgin. Giv and all heroes went before the king despondently. Gorgin was terrified, and immediately went to Kay Khosrow. He gave the king the boars' teeth, bowed, and prayed for him. Kay Khosrow heard the whole story from Gorgin, but it made no sense. He knew that he was lying, and said, "For your mistake, your head should be removed from your body; but I don't want to commit a sin before God. I shall put you in shackles and throw you in a cell." He called Giv and said, "I shall find Bijan. If I fail, I will bring the Cup of Jamshid in the month of Farvardin, and look into it to find where he is." Khosrow sent his riders in every direction to find Bijan. They searched for a long time and found no sign of him.

Newroz (Persian new year) arrived, and Kay Khosrow saw that Giv was miserable. He demanded the Cup of Jamshid, which he put before himself and looked at. He saw Bijan in shackles inside a well, and the daughter of a king looking after him. He gave Giv the good news, and gathered the heroes and asked, "Who will go to help Bijan?" "This only Rostam is capable of," all heroes said in unison. Kay Khosrow immediately wrote a letter to Rostam. Giv took the letter and went to Zabolestan.

Zaal received him until Rostam returned from hunting. Giv told him about Bijan's disappearance and how he was seen in the Cup of Jamshid. Rostam read the letter and wept for Bijan. He assured Giv that he would not climb down Rakhsh until he had found Bijan. They made merry in the palace for a few days, and then returned to Kay Khosrow in Iran's capital. The king welcomed him with the elites and the army. They went to Kay Khosrow's palace and talked for some time. When Gorgin was notified of Rostam's arrival, he sent him a message that,

"O Hero of the World, if you vouch for me by the king; I shall come to Turan with you and spare no efforts in freeing Bijan." "I shall not name the name of a sly fox such as yourself before the king." answered Rostam, "If we find Bijan alive, you will be freed. Otherwise, I shall unleash my wrath upon you in revenge."

Rostam mounted his horse to go to Turan; but he felt sorry for Gorgin and told Kay Khosrow, "If his majesty sees fit, he could send Gorgin with me, for he knows where Bijan disappeared and is thinking of redeeming himself." The king did not reject him, and forgave Gorgin. Kay Khosrow sent a vast army with Rostam. "The solution is deception," argued Rostam, "And now is not the time for war." He wore a merchant's attire, and departed with much gold accompanied by several heroes, such as Gorgin, Zengeh, Gostaham, Gorazeh, Farhad, and Roham. They were heading towards Turan. When they reached the border, Rostam stopped the army near the border, and told them to be ready for war on his command. Then, he and several heroes entered Turan disguised as merchants. They approached Khotan (in China), and its people gathered around to watch their caravan. Piran, returning from a hunt, saw them.

Rostam prepared and gave precious gifts to Piran, but he did not recognize him, and asked his name and origins. Rostam replied, "I am a merchant here from Iran to sell my goods in

Turan." Upon seeing his gifts, Piran ordered him to be left alone and allowed free trade. Manijeh was informed, and came to Rostam barefoot and told him of Bijan's imprisonment. "Get away from me," Rostam hollered at her, "I don't know Kay Khosrow and Rostam, and have no business with Bijan." Manijeh begged, and Rostam ordered to prepare food. They dined, and Rostam asked his questions. Finally, Manijeh asked him to tell the Iranian heroes of Bijan's imprisonment. Rostam asked for a barbecued chicken, wrapped it in bread, put his ring inside, and gave it to Manijeh, saying, "Take this food to that poor soul in the well." Manijeh returned to the well and dropped the food through the hole. "Where did you get all this food?" asked Bijan.

Manijeh told him about the Iranian merchants. Bijan started to eat and saw Rostam's ring. He was ecstatic, and told Manijeh everything he had grasped, "Ask him if he is Rakhsh's lord." Manijeh came to Rostam and gave Bijan's message. "Tell her that, yes, I am Rakhsh's lord," said Rostam, "and have come from Iran to liberate you." He then said, "collect plenty of firewood around the well, and light it at night." Manijeh returned to Bijan with his message, and gathered firewood. At night, she made a massive fire. Rostam saw the light, went toward it, and reached the well. He saw the stone of Akvan Div on the well. The seven heroes tried their best but couldn't remove the stone. Rostam dismounted his horse, uttered the Lord's name, raised the stone, and launched it towardt China's forests. Then, he hung his lasso into the well, pulled Bijan out, and asked him to forgive Gorgin. He agreed, and Rostam unshackled him and gave him expensive attire to wear. They sent Manijeh to the border with Iran, where the army was stationed. Gorgin asked Bijan for forgiveness. They decided to do something to humiliate Afrasiab, and entered his palace. As Afrasiab was getting ready for bed, he found all his soldiers headless, and heard Rostam from across the hallway, "I'm Rostam of Zabol. I lifted the stone of Akvan Div from the well, and freed Bijan." "You should have fought me like a man," said Bijan, "Not thrown me in a well in shackles." He pulled Afrasiab by the collar. Scared witless, Afrasiab called his soldiers, and fled at once.

The heroes gathered everything in the palace as well as his jewelry and horses, and returned to the Iranian border. Rostam ordered them to prepare for war. Manijeh was sitting in the camp and waiting for them. There was a storm in the city of Turan, as people came to Afrasiab's palace and saw it empty. The king ordered the army to prepare for war with Iran. The two armies lined up against each other, and the army of Turan initiated the fighting. Rostam attacked in every direction, and cut off many heads. Many of Turan's soldiers escaped, and Rostam returned to Iran with the spoils of war. The king was elated with the news and celebrated his return. He also gave Rostam many gifts, which he shared with the elders. Kay Khosrow called Bijan, and asked him about the journey's hardships. He told him everything. Kay Khosrow gave Manijeh many dresses, things, gifts, and maids, married them, and asked Bijan to treat her right.

# The Seven Trials of Esfandiar

Esfandiar was the son of king Gushtasp and Katayun (the daughter of Rome's Caesar). Gushtasp made a condition for Esfandiar that if he intended to rule Iran, he should go to Roein Castle and free his sisters from Turan. So Esfandiar came to Balkh and asked for Gorgsar, the imprisoned hero of Turan. Then, he gave him four glasses of wine, and asked of his arrival to Roein Castle, "If you tell me the truth and show the way, I shall appoint you the king of Turan after my reign, and will leave your family and children in peace. But if you lie; I shall split you in half with my dagger." "I will tell you nothing but the truth," answered Gorgsar, "Roein Castle is located on the Iran-Turan border, and there is a constant army presence. There are three ways there. One way, which takes three months, is very lush, pleasant, and easy to traverse, and passes through a city. The other path, taken in two months, passes through a dry desert and is no place to rest. The third path, taken in a week, is scattered with wolves, lions, and dragons, and it is the mountain pass."

Esfandiar reflected and chose the one-week path. He then told Gorgsar, "I shall take you with me to show me the way." "This is the path of the seven trials," said Gorgsar, "In the first trial, you will face two giant male and female wolves with elephant-like teeth." With an army, they departed to Roein Castle. Upon reaching the first trial, Esfandiar assigned his brother, Peshotan, to watch the army, wore combat attire, and went into the forest of gigantic wild wolves. He put the arrow in the bow and hit them. Then, he unsheathed his sword and tore them apart. Esfandiar then climbed down his horse and prayed to God.

Peshotan followed Esfandiar with the army, and saw him praying. Afterwards, they celebrated. Esfandiar called Gorgsar, gave him three glasses of wine, and asked, "Tell me about the second trial." "In the second trial," said Gorgsar, "a fierce lion will attack you, which a whale cannot withstand." Esfandiar scoffed, asked the army to remain in the camp at night, and gave Peshotan the guard duty. At dawn, he went to the lion's den. He saw a lion and a lioness that were very fierce and strong. First, the lion attacked him, and Esfandiar tore it in two with his sword. The lioness was scared to see its mate dead; so it attacked him, and Esfandiar smashed his sword against her head. The earth became red with the blood of the two animals. Esfandiar waded into water to wash himself, and thanked God. The army came to him.

He came to the royal court, dined, and demanded Gorgsar. He gave him three glasses of wine and asked, "What will I face tomorrow in the third trial?" "In this trial," he said, "You will see a fire-breathing dragon as big as a mountain. I think you should return and forget about fighting." Esfandiar ordered to collect wood, build a chest, and put large blades all around. First, he entered the chest to test it. Early in the morning, he entrusted the army to Peshotan, wore armor, and sat inside the chest. Two horses were dragging the chest up the mountain to the dragon. The dragon saw the horses from afar, flew toward them, and devoured the horses and the chest. The blades pierced its mouth and it bled; it could neither swallow nor throw up. Esfandiar emerged and stabbed the dragon's brain from inside its mouth. The dragon collapsed to the ground, and the tar from its mouth made Esfandiar unconscious. Peshotan saw them fighting from a distance and thought that Esfandiar was dead, so he came near and sprinkled rosewater on his head. Esfandiar woke up, washed up, and thanked God.

The army praised him. Gorgsar was deeply troubled to see Esfandiar alive. That night, they held a feast and brought Gorgsar. Esfandiar gave him three glasses of wine, and asked about the fourth trial. "In the fourth trial," said Gorgsar, "A sorceress named Ghoul, who can turn desert into the sea, will come to you. I ask you to return." Esfandiar laughed. At dawn, he gave Peshotan control over the army, and headed to the land of the sorceress. She was nowhere to be seen. The weather was mild, the earth was lush and flowery, and he sat down to play a tune. The sorceress heard his melody, so she turned herself into a beautiful young woman and came to Esfandiar. Esfandiar gave her a drink, and put the chain that Zoroaster had put around his arm and from which he received his strength, around the woman's neck. The sorceress could not withstand the prayer, and immediately returned to her original old form. Esfandiar struck his head with his dagger, and she died.

 Peshotan and the army praised him. Esfandiar prayed, and a banquet was cast. He gave Gorgsar three glasses of wine, and asked about the fifth trial. "In this trial," said Gorgsar, "You have a tough task ahead. You must fight a Simorgh that is as strong as an elephant. It has two children, and will do anything to protect them. You can return with your life." Esfandiar contemplated until morning, and asked for another chest. At dawn, he prayed to God, sat in his chest, and two horses dragged it.

Upon seeing the chest, the Simorgh descended like a panther and hit it with its wings. The blades penetrated its wings, and blood poured forth from its body. The two chicks saw it and ran away. Esfandiar came out of the chest, killed the Simorgh, and then praised God. Peshotan and the army found him, and saw the ground covered with Simorgh's feathers. They all commended him except Gorgsar, who became pale and trembled. By Esfandiar's order, the banquet was cast and Gorgsar was called.

He gave him three cups of wine, and asked about the sixth trial. "You won this time with the Lord's blessing," said Gorgsar, "But in the sixth trial, fighting and swordplay will not save you. There will be a snowstorm, and you will lose your way. Then, you will reach a desert of thirty parasangs covered with hot stones, and you will not see any birds, serpents, or even a drop of water. Following that, there is Roein Dezh, which no four-legged animal can enter. A hundred-thousand soldiers cannot push through, and it houses the provisions for several years."

The Iranians noticed Gorgsar's cynicism, and the elders complained to Esfandiar that their deaths were nigh and they had no escape. "You return," decreed Esfandiar, "I'll do this alone. My son and my brother will suffice." They apologized and stayed with him. The morning breeze whisked by, followed by a storm from the mountain and substantial snowfall. It snowed for three days and three nights. Esfandiar told his army, "The solution to this does not involve force and swordplay. We should all pray for the Lord to free us from this disaster." The Iranians prayed as one for three days, and the snow and cold disappeared. Esfandiar ordered the horses to be loaded with plenty of water and food, and went forth into the desert. Ahead, the horses were stuck in a deep sea.

Esfandiar called Gorgsar and said, "You said there would be a desert, and this is a sea." "This water is very salty," said Gorgsar, "and cannot be used." Esfandiar realized that Gorgsar's heart was filled with hate, and ordered the army to release the water and the provisions into the sea immediately; and he pulled the horses from the mud on his own. Esfandiar asked Gorgsar to move the army across the sea in return for the kingdom of Turan after they reached Roein Dezh. Gorgsar moved the army across the shallow spring. Then, he cursed at the Iranians, and Esfandiar cut him in half with his sword. He became invulnerable after crossing the sea, and they reached Roein Dezh.

He surveyed his surroundings, captured two Tur soldiers atop the guard tower, and questioned them about the fort before killing them. Esfandiar and Peshotan sought solitude in the royal court, and he said, "This fort is very robust, and it cannot be captured through war. I shall enter the fort disguised as a merchant. Appoint a guard for the army, and whenever you see smoke and fire in the fort, know that it is me." Then, a hundred ginger camels were brought. He loaded them with textile and dinars, and they entered the fort with a hundred and sixty heroes. When Turan's elites heard of the Iranian merchants' presence, they came to watch.

Esfandiar went to the king to get his reward. He took some gifts for him and presented them to Arjasp. He introduced himself as Kharad, the son of a Turkish father and an Iranian mother, and a merchant trading between Iran and Turan.

He asked the king for safety to continue trading in that country. Arjasp agreed and promised that no harm would come to him. Esfandiar built a hut and put his items on display. There were many buyers. Once again, Esfandiar brought many crowns and gifts to Arjasp. The king asked about Esfandiar, and he said that he had received his father's wrath and was taking on the seven trials to prove his heroism. Arjasp guffawed and belittled Esfandiar.

The next morning, Kharad (Esfandiar) was busy trading in the market when he saw two sisters carrying water jugs on their backs. Esfandiar concealed his face. They came to him, begged for help, and inquired about Iranian heroes and the king of Iran. Esfandiar yelled to drive them away, "I am but a merchant and do not know these people." Homay, Esfandiar's sister, recognized him, but didn't bat an eyelid. Esfandiar felt ill-at-ease and said, "Be patient for a few more days until I remove this dishonor." Then, he went to Arjasp and said, "When we waded through the deep sea, I asked God for assistance in return for holding a feast upon entry to Roein Dezh. Now, I want to hold this celebration and invite the elders. But my house is too small. I want to hold this event on the fort's roof with your permission. Arjasp was euphoric, and gave permission for the celebration. Esfandiar ordered to gather firewood to set alight the roof of the fort. All of Turan's elders came to the party and drank until they were befuddled. Esfandiar lit the firewood; the army watch spotted the fire, and came near the wall by Peshoten's order. There was a rumor of Esfandiar's attack inside the fort. While drunk, the king ordered Kahram to go to war. Thus, Tarkhan left the fort with a thousand cavalry to fight the Iranian army.

The army of Turan was pitted against Iran, and the fighting commenced. Nooshazar, son of Esfandiar, pursued Tarkhan, and ultimately slit him in half. Kahram, another hero of Turan, attacked the heart of the Iranian army, and then escaped toward the fort. He told Afrasiab, his father, of his defeat. Afrasiab ordered the entire army to leave the fort to confront the Iranians. Upon seeing the fort vacated, Esfandiar asked for food, and prayed. He wore his armor, and divided the heroes into three groups. He put one group inside the fort to kill whomever they saw; he put the second group facing the gate to watch for entries and exits. The third group was tasked with killing the drunkard guests on the roof. Then, he came to Arjasp with twenty fighters. He saw his sisters, Bahafarid and Homay, embraced them, and sent them to his royal court. Arjasp, who had just woken up, wore combat attire, and engaged Esfandiar in battle. Arjasp was wounded and fell down. Esfandiar parted his head from his body, and took his daughters and wives captive. He assigned several guards for the gate to stop Turks from entering. Then, they threw Arjasp's head toward Turan's army from the top of the fort. The army dispersed, his two children came forward weeping, and they attacked the Iranian army.

There was a mass of dead bodies around the fort. Kahram wrestled with Esfandiar, but he grabbed Kahram's belt and pounded him to the ground. He tied his two hands and sent him to his army. After killing all of Turan's heroes, he put two gallows on top of the fort, and executed Arjasp's two sons, Andriman and Kahram. He then wrote a letter to Gushtasp, and asked permission for his return. He explained that he had avenged the blood of his thirty-eight brothers and freed his sisters. He took all the treasure in the fort, set it on fire, and sent the army back to Iran through the desert, then returned to the Seven Trials for hunting and recreation. He had three sons who went to Iran with Turan's treasures. There was a celebration in Gushtasp's palace. Esfandiar returned and embraced his father. His father praised him extensively, and asked about his sufferings along the journey; and Esfandiar diligently answered all of his questions.

# Rostam and Esfandiar

Some time passed. One day, Esfandiar returned from the king's palace to his mother Katayun, downhearted, and said, "The king is unfair to me. He had promised me to give me the throne after I slay Arjasp and liberate my sisters, but he didn't. If he doesn't live by his vow, I shall assume the throne without his consent and become king." Katayun was troubled and said, "My son, your father's only strength over you is the king's crown. The entire army and treasury belong to you, and you are the pride of Iranians. After your father's death, you will become the king. Therefore, you would be wise to be obedient."

 Katayun was anxious about him. Esfandiar drank for two days and two nights, and Gushtasp was notified. He immediately called his sage, Jamasp, and asked, "Tell me, what does the future hold for Esfandiar? Will he sit on the throne?" Jamasp looked at the charts, his eyes were filled with tears, and he began to curse himself and fate, "Esfandiar will be killed in Zabolestan by Rostam's hand." "What if I give him the reigns?" asked Gushtasp, "If I don't send him to Zabol, will he be safe?" "No one shall be spared from death," said Jamasp.

The next day, the king sat on the throne, and Esfandiar went to him and reminded him of his promise. He named everything he had done for the king and what Gushtasp had done to him, and added, "Despite it all, I ripped my leash and came to you when you needed me. I did not flout your commands. Now, what is your excuse for barring me from the throne?" "There is none like you in this world," said Gushtasp, "Except Rostam, son of Zaal, who ignored Kavus' command. I have no one to fight him. I want you to go to Sistan, trick him and Faramarz, and bring them to me in chains. If you accomplish this, I shall give you the throne." Esfandiar tried to remind him of all that Rostam had done for Iranians. Gushtasp said, "If you want to become king, this is my condition." "You don't wish to give me the crown," said Esfandiar, "and are using Rostam as an excuse. But I am your servant and shall do as you wish." Gushtasp said, "Take an army with battle-hardened fighters." "An army is of no use to me in this battle," said Esfandiar.

He returned to his veranda enraged. Katayun was upset, went to him, and advised him against fighting Rostam, "Your father is old and you are young. The entire army considers you to be the king. There are places other than Sistan for you to display your courage. Do not make me miserable, and listen to me. Rostam is a decent man, and you should not do wrong by him." "How could I disobey the king," said Esfandiar, "He has ordered me to go to Zabol and bring Rostam in a chain." Katayun was weeping blood and trying to persuade her son against his mission. The next day, Esfandiar went to Zabol on a horse; but the leading camel sat down and would not move no matter what.

Esfandiar took it as a bad omen and ordered it to have its head cut off. Then, they went to Hirmand and pitched a court. They had a feast and brought musicians. He told his comrades, "The nation of Iran stands for Rostam's bravery. We should send him a message, and ask him to surrender. If he is not stubborn, I will bring him no harm." He called Bahman (his son), and said, "Wear an expensive attire and put on a king's crown. Take ten respected mobads with you via Rostam's special path, and state Gushtasp's demands. Ask him to surrender without resistance, and promise him that no harm will come to him. Remind him that he owes everything to our ancestors. Say, "When our father took the throne, you didn't go to him, didn't write a letter, and did not prove your servitude; He holds a grudge against you, his heart is troubled by you, and he has demanded you in a chain. You have always done right by Iran and Iranians, so heed the king's command. I vow to make the king regret his order, and will make him return you to greatness. Peshotan is my witness, and I will remain faithful to my word. You, Zavareh, Faramarz, Zaal, and Rudabeh should come to me so that I may take you to the capital in chains."

Bahman received the message and headed to Hirmand. The scout watched him, and Zaal came to welcome him. Bahman did not recognize Zaal and said, "Farmer, where can I find Rostam, son of Zaal?" Zaal introduced himself and said, "Rostam is on a hunt; come and join us until he returns." and paid his respects. Zaal made a courier named Shirkhoun accompany him to Rostam. On his way to the hunting ground, Bahman saw Rostam holding a tree and barbecuing a zebra. Bahman threw down a rock from the top of the mountain. Zavareh saw and tried to stop it, but Rostam prevented him. When the rock came near, he stopped it with his heel.

Bahman was distressed and wondered, "We should be lenient with this lion and not seek war." Rostam saw him and asked his name and origin. Bahman stepped off his horse and introduced himself. Rostam embraced him, and cast a banquet where they conversed. Bahman was shocked by his foods and drinks. Thereafter, they gave him Esfandiar's message. Upon hearing his message, Rostam said, "We both worship God and are safe from evil. I will come to you now to hear the king. Is the shackle and chain the compensation for my services and struggles?! No one has ever seen me in shackles. Come with me and be my guests, and let the enemies be blinded with hate. Then, we shall go to the king, and I shall soften his rage. Tell Esfandiar what I said."

After hearing Rostam, Bahman departed to Esfandiar's court with the mobad. Rostam asked Faramarz to go to Zaal-e-Dastan and prepare to receive Esfandiar, "If he changes his mind, I shall give him all my treasures and dinars, and if he persists on his unfounded claims, I shall put him to the ground with my lasso." Zavareh, Rostam and Zaal went to the Hirmand River to greet Esfandiar. Bahman went to Esfandiar, told him everything he had seen, and said, "Rostam wants to go and see the king of his own accord."

Esfandiar was disappointed with Bahman and humiliated him before the others, "They are right to say that children should not be sent to do the business of grown-ups. He sought to deceive you." He then told Peshotan, "Rostam wants war and will not surrender." He ordered to have one hundred of his best cavalry to come to him near Hirmand River. After seeing him, Tahamtan went into the water on foot and saluted him. He assured him that he was not seeking deception and lies. Esfandiar climbed down his horse, embraced Rostam, and started to sing his praises. Rostam asked him to be his guest and Esfandiar responded, "I wished to do this, but the king has ordered to not hesitate in Zabol.

You should tie yourself up and let me take you to the king. You will remain imprisoned as long as the king of Iran is alive. After I assume the throne, I shall return you to Zabol with pomp and circumstance." "This is a disgrace that will haunt me forever. I will obey you, but no one will see me a captive alive." "Peshotan has received the king›s order," said Esfandiar, "and I have no choice but to oblige. I will ignore our camaraderie and fight you if you do not surrender. But if you want to, we will sit together and rejoice today." "Then, I shall go and bring the means of a reception," said Rostam. He returned to his veranda and told Zaal the entire story. When Rostam left, Esfandiar told Peshotan, "We have a difficult task ahead of us. I have no business in Rostam's veranda and cannot be merry with him." "Do not go to war with him," said Peshotan, "For you will fail to take him to the capital in a chain." "I cannot stand against the king of Iran," said Esfandiar, "For my life and the afterlife will be ruined."

"I ask you to choose the best," said Peshotan. Before the commander could cast a banquet, he spoke of previous wars.

At the same time, Rostam prepared for the feast and awaited Esfandiar, but no one came. Rostam told his brother, "Saddle up Rakhsh so that I may go to Esfandiar and see why he has ignored what I said." He rode Rakhsh, took the cow mace, and went to Hirmand. Esfandiar's army complimented Rostam and murmured, "The king has lost all semblance of reason to try to fight such a hero." Rostam came to Esfandiar and complained to him. Esfandiar scoffed, saying, "I was supposed to meet Zaal at dawn. You didn't need to trouble yourself and came here. Now join me for a meal." Then, he ordered Bahman to bring Rostam a golden chair.

Esfandiar reminded Rostam of Zaal's history, that his ancestors accepted him and gave him treasure. Rostam was troubled and defended his father and grandfather. He reminded Esfandiar of his paternal and maternal ancestors, and recounted Saam and Zaal's services to Iranian kings, then spoke of his wars. Thereafter, they wined and dined, and Esfandiar told him of his accomplishments and services, and his lineage (Esfandiar attempted to humiliate Rostam and convince him that he is but a servant, and his status as the hero of Sistan was owed to his ancestors.) Finally, he spoke to Rostam of his suffering, the Seven Trials, and taking over Roein Dezh.

Meanwhile, Rostam spoke of his Seven Labors and the Battle of Hamavaran, and said, "Was I not there, Gushtasp's crown would be on someone else's head, and you had nothing to be proud of today." Esfandiar fumed at Rostam's harsh words. He held Rostam's hand, pressed it, and returned the favor. "O renowned Rostam," said Esfandiar, "Today we dine, and tomorrow we shall fight. I will then tie your hand, and take you to the king. "You have not seen men fight," scoffed Rostam, "Tomorrow, I shall hug you on your horse, take you to Zaal, seat you on the throne, and put the crown on your head. I shall give you all of my riches and send Gushtasp gifts as thanks."

They celebrated and made merry that day. Before leaving, Rostam asked Esfandiar to forget about fighting, and be his guest. Then, he proposed that they meet the king in the capital and let Rostam talk him out of it. "If I win or he puts me in shackles," Rostam contemplated, "Both are undesirable, and people will not remember our good names. If I kill him, I shall be ashamed before the kings for having killed a young prince, and people›s curses will be upon me. If he slays me, the name of Dastan will vanish." "King," he said, "Do not be defeated by your youth, do not bring you and myself harm, and do not make me guilty before the Lord." "You are saying this because of your old age and frailty," said Esfandiar, "You want to leave for posterity a good name." Rostam was troubled and left. Esfandiar prepared his weapons of war. Peshotan tried to extinguish his rage and hate and talk him out of fighting Rostam;

but Esfandiar's heart was filled with pride and would not hear. Rostam asked his brother to prepare his weapons. Zavareh also tried to persuade him against fighting. "I will not kill him," said Rostam, "I want to bring him with honor and seat him on the throne."

At dawn, Rostam wore his combat armor and went to Hirmand with Zavareh. He asked him to hold the army and said, "I will try to fight him face to face. Neither you nor the army should interfere." Then, he called Esfandiar to fight. Esfandiar laughed, saying, "I woke up today hoping to fight you." He wore his armor and told Peshotan, "He is alone, and I shall go alone." The two heroes faced off. "If you seek battle and bloodshed," said Rostam, "Let me send you Zabol's cavalry." Esfandiar fumed and thought that Rostam was being devious, then said, "I always go to battle alone. If you need help, make the call." They vowed not to let anyone else interfere.

First, they fought with spears, but they snapped and their combat attires were torn. Then, they attacked each other with swords and wounded each other and their horses. Not even the maces could outlast the fighting. Rostam and Esfandiar reached for each other's belts and tried to raise each other from the saddle, but they both failed. Meanwhile, Zavareh became worried for Rostam. He pitted his army against Esfandiar's, and cursed at them. Nooshazar, Esfandiar's son, was irked, and answered, "Esfandiar has not allowed us to fight. But if you insist, I will make you regret it." Zavareh attacked Esfandiar's army and killed many. Nooshazar galloped toward Rostam's army. Alway, one of Rostam's heroes, attacked Nooshazar, who cleaved him in half with his sword. Zavareh was livid to see the young hero die and killed Nooshazar with a spear.

His brother, Mehrnoosh, wept for him, and attacked Rostam's army. Faramarz struggled with him and managed to pull him off his horse. Bahman, Esfandiar's other son, immediately went into battle and announced that Sistan's army had killed his two brothers. Esfandiar told Rostam, "You lowlife, is this how you honor your vows?! Do you not fear the Lord and the Day of Judgment? Two of your dogs killed my two sons."

They both returned to their camps. Rostam was perturbed and trembled in pain and torment. He swore that his army had done so in violation of his command; and said, "I will bring you my brother and Faramarz with their hands tied." "I will avenge them and make your army suffer," said Esfandiar. They attacked each other with arrows. Rostam and Rakhsh were wounded, but Rostam's arrow failed to hit Esfandiar. Rostam went on foot, and Rakhsh returned home alone. Esfandiar scoffed and said, "Where is your chivalry and bravery? You flee like an old fox?"

After seeing Rakhsh, Zavareh came to Rostam and tried to give him his horse. "Go to Zaal and find a solution," said Rostam, "Treat Rakhsh also. I will join you if I survive." "I shall take you to the king in a chain," said Esfandiar, "Ask the Lord for forgiveness." "The night has come," said Rostam, "and it is not the time for fighting. Let us return and make merry, and we shall resume fighting tomorrow. If you demand it, I shall deliver Zavareh and Faramarz." "You are a great man," said Esfandiar, "and I shall let you rest the night. Deal with those two as you see fit." When Esfandiar left, Rostam waded into the river, washed himself, and prayed to God.

Esfandiar and Peshotan received a golden casket, washed the dead, put them inside, and sent them back to Gushtasp with a message. Rostam entered his veranda bearing many wounds from arrows. Zavareh and Faramarz wept to see him and Rudabeh pulled her hair. They took off his clothes, he ordered to treat Rakhsh, and Zaal rubbed its wounds with ointment. "There is no point to grieving, for this is fate. I fought great battles and won in all, and I shall not give in to Esfandiar. I thank God that night came and I was freed from him." "We need help from Simorgh," said Zaal. Zaal put the Simorgh›s feather in fire, and the Simorgh appeared instantly. Zaal praised it and discussed his problem. He then sent it after Rostam and Rakhsh. "If Rostam is defeated," said Zaal, "They will destroy Sistan."

Simorgh caressed Rostam's wounds with its feathers and said, "Douse one of my feathers in milk and put it on your and Rakhsh's wounds. Why do you seek to fight Esfandiar? Don't you know that he is immortal?!" "The king has asked me to go to him as a captive," said Rostam, "And this I cannot accept." "Iran is entrusted to a king like him," said Simorgh, "It is a shame for a king like Esfandiar to be slain. I will tell you a secret. Whoever spills Esfandiar's blood will live miserably and die in agony." "Dying with a good name is better than the humiliation of capture," said Rostam. Simorgh raised Rostam and headed to the desert, then said, "Pick a manna tree branch that is wide on one end and thin on the other. Put it on fire and sharpen it like an arrow. When Esfandiar comes to fight, try to persuade him against it; and if he doesn't agree; put the poisoned arrow in his eye." Simorgh flew away.

Dawn broke. Rostam wore his fighting attire and prayed to God, then attended Esfandiar's court and called him to fight. Esfandiar told Peshotan, "I didn't expect Rostam to recover and be ready for battle so early. I had heard Zaal-e-Dastan was a wizard, but I never believed it and thought it far-fetched." "You are not well today," said Peshotan, "Perhaps you didn't sleep last night?" Esfandiar protected himself with armor, came to Rostam, and threatened him. "Fear God and do not talk of war," said Rostam, "I have come to you to make amends, yet you still disrespect me. Come to my home and enjoy my treasure. I will accompany you to the king. If the time is right, he will put me to death." "Do not deceive me," Esfandiar retorted, "If you are honest, tie yourself up and come here." "My king!" declared Rostam, "Let go of war so that the world may not utter my name in disgrace." "You are trying to bamboozle me," said Esfandiar, "If you do not surrender, only war and bloodshed will remain. Do not makeup excuses."

Rostam realized that his words would not move Esfandiar. He put the arrow doused in rosewater in the bow, and prayed. "Hero of Sistan!" declared Esfandiar, "Are you not tired of fighting with the bow?" Then, he started firing Rostam realized that his words would not move Esfandiar. He put the arrow doused in rosewater in the bow, and prayed. "Hero of Sistan!" declared Esfandiar, "Are you not tired of fighting with the bow?" Then, he started firing Esfandiar›s eye. Esfandiar collapsed from his horse, and his blood flowed on the ground. "You were the one who considered yourself immortal?" said Rostam, "Witness how you fell with but one arrow!"

Esfandiar was unconscious for some time but woke up, sat up, and pulled the arrow from his eye. Bahman and Peshotan were informed, and they joined the fighting on foot. They poured dirt on their heads and tore their robes when they saw him. "Curse this crown and throne," moaned Peshotan, "for bringing death to a lionheart like you." Esfandiar consoled him, "We are not eternal, and are destined to depart this world. I tried to execute the Lord›s command. But it wasn›t Rostam who killed me. It was the manna arrow and the sorcery of Simorgh and Zaal." Rostam wept and said, "I have never seen a hero like Esfandiar. I sought help from Simorgh since I was unable to take him on. I would not have done so had he let go of war." Zaal and Faramarz came to Esfandiar weeping. "I will weep for you," said Zaal, "For he who spills Esfandiar's blood shall become a wretch and live on in agony." "You were the scapegoat," said Esfandiar, "In fact, it was my father who wanted to end me. Now I ask you to nurture my son Bahman. Be a father to him, and teach him whatever is necessary. Jamasp predicted that he would become the king of Iran."

Rostam stood up, put his hand on his heart, and promised that he would raise Bahman fittingly. Then, he told Peshotan, "When I die, take the army and return to your father. Tell him you became king and inherited the world's riches. In the afterlife, we shall be granted an audience before the Lord and answer. Tell my mother not to grieve and weep, for she will join me soon. Tell my sister and wife that my father brought upon this evil for the sake of the crown, and Gushtasp did wrong by me." He surrendered himself to the Creator.

Rostam, Peshotan, and Bahman all wept and tore their outfits. They adorned an iron coffin, put Esfandiar inside, and returned him to the capital in glory. Bahman stayed with Rostam in Zabol, weeping blood. When the news reached Gushtasp, he tore apart his attire. The name of Esfandiar echoed throughout Iran. The elders loathed Gushtasp and said, "O villain, did you send Esfandiar to Zabol to be slain for the sake of the throne?! You did so to stay king?! Shame on you." His mother and sister left the palace barefoot, weeping, and embraced Peshotan and asked him to open the coffin. As the women were dragging their nails on his arms, Peshotan wept in agony. At last, he opened the coffin. They saw Esfandiar's handsome face and calmed down, then pet his horse.

After seeing Esfandiar in the coffin, there was a commotion in the army. Peshotan came to his father but did not pay his respects and said, "Fate has turned its back against you, and you should pay for Esfandiar's blood. You caused your own son's downfall for the crown. The entire nation of Iran is your enemy, and you will not have the throne for an eternity. With your vain remarks, a worthy king was slain." Behafarid and Homay went to their father weeping, and denounced him while Peshotan comforted his mother. The nation of Iran mourned Esfandiar for a year.

# Bahman

Back in Zabol, Bahman was busy dining and hunting. Rostam taught him statecraft, and loved him even more than his own son. One day, he wrote a letter to Gushtasp, saying, "As Peshotan is my witness, I spared no effort in advising Esfandiar against fighting. I would even give him my entire territory and treasure. It was his fate, and my heart was filled with pain and sorrow. Now, his son is with me, and I taught him all there is to being a king. I want you to accept him."

The king received the letter, and Peshotan vouched for its truthfulness. The king rejoiced, and replied to Rostam. Jamasp knew that Bahman was destined to be the king, and told Gushtasp, "Send a letter to Bahman and call him to your side." The king did so. Rostam gave Bahman all the wealth he needed, and dispatched him to the capital. Gushtasp saw him and tears flowed from his eyes. He was a wise believer, capable of war and hunting, and a hero like Esfandiar. Gushtasp consoled his sorrow for Rostam with Bahman, and entrusted the throne to him after death.

# The Death of Rostam

Zaal had a son named Shaghad from his maid. Astronomers predicted his fate to be ill and said, "He will bring an end to Saam's bloodline." Zaal was dejected, and sent him to the king of Kabul. The king of Kabul grew fond of him, and gave him much treasure. He then married his daughter to him to bring a noble child. One day, Shaghad asked the king, "Why do you feel obliged to pay a golden cow's leather to Rostam as royalty? I am his brother and your son-in-law, but he is not ashamed of receiving royalty. Let's trap him and be rid of him" Shaghad didn't sleep until morning. He contemplated and said, "Let's hold a massive ceremony where you curse me. I will sulk, go to Zabol, and complain to Rostam and Zaal. Rostam will come to you for retribution. Choose a hunting ground, and dig several wells to fit Rostam and Rakhsh. Put tall spears inside the wells."

The king of Kabul did so, and humiliated Shaghad in the ceremony, and demeaned him worse than Rostam. Shaghad complained to Rostam and Zaal. Rostam started to Kabul to kill the king and enthrone Shaghad. Rostam wanted to go to Kabul with his army, but Shaghad stopped him and advised him to choose peace instead of war. Rostam climbed Rakhsh and went to Kabul. The king removed his crown and apologized. Then, he held a ceremony, and they took Rostam to the hunting ground. Shaghad and the army dispersed. Rakhsh approached the well, sensed the smell of fresh soil, and stood still. Rostam tried to push on, but Rakhsh was stationary since it was between two wells. Rostam whipped his steed, and they both fell into the well and the daggers and blades punctured their bodies, and he knew that it was Shaghad›s handiwork. He dragged himself to the edge of the well and saw Shaghad. He asked him for two arrows and a bow to be able to defend himself against animals. Shaghad happily obliged, and hid behind an old tree in fear of Rostam. Rostam put an arrow in the bow and launched it at Shaghad, impaling him on the tree. After ۱۰۷ years of chivalry, Rostam left this world. When they heard the news, Zavareh and Faramarz went to Kabul, washed their bodies with musk and amber, and attacked Kabul with a large army to avenge Rostam.

# Ardashir

Ardashir was enthroned in Baghdad and put on the crown. His likeness closely resembled Gushtasp. The king sent a representative to every country to know his enemies. He spread justice around the nation, and made the country prosper. Ardashir chose the daughter of Artabanus (Bahram, the Parthian king) as his spouse. Two of his sons fled to India, and his other two sons were imprisoned. Artabanus' eldest son, Bahram, sent poison to his sisters and said, "If your heart is still with your brothers and you intend to avenge our father from Ardashir, make him drink this."

One day, Ardashir left the palace on a hunt. Artabanus' daughter returned to him, poured the poison in a yellow glass, made a drink with sugar and water, and gave it to the king. The cup fell out of the king's hand and broke, and the girl trembled. The king became suspicious of her, and ordered the rest of the drink to be fed to four domestic chickens. The birds died immediately. The king called the vizier and asked, "What is the punishment for those who betray their king?" "Her head should be cut off," the vizier answered. The king ordered to behead the daughter of Artabanus. The girl told the mobad, "I am pregnant from the king. Wait for my baby to be born, then kill me." The mobad delivered her message to the king, who ordered her to ignore her plea and execute her. "The king has no sons," the mobad pondered, "I should wait for his son to be born before I kill her. If the king has no successor, the enemies will take over the country." He prepared a place and kept the girl there in secret. After some time, she gave birth to a handsome boy.

The mobad named him Shapur and kept him away from prying eyes for seven years. One day, he saw the king crying, and asked the reason. The king said, "I am now fifty-one, and have no son to succeed me. After me, my enemies will inherit my crown." "If you guarantee my safety," conditioned the mobad, "I will tell you a secret." He then told him the entire story. Ardashir was ecstatic and said, "Bring him and a hundred other boys of his age in uniforms to play polo. Let me see if I grow fond of my son and recognize him."

Mobad did as the king commanded. Shapur's strikes on the ball were better than the rest. Ardashir entered the arena with several associates, then told a servant, "Go and throw the polo ball at me to see who dares to take it. He is certainly my son." The servant obliged. The boys ran after the ball; but they all stopped when they reached Ardashir. Shapur came forward, took the ball, and threw it toward the children. The king's cavalry hugged the boy and raised him in the air. They praised and kissed him, and buried him under a pile of gold and jewelry. The king raised him, seated him on his throne, and ordered him to bring the daughter of Artabanus. He forgave her, and entrusted Shapur to experienced tutors to teach him knowledge and craft.

Then, the king ordered to mint a new coin with the name of Ardashir inscribed on one side, and the name of his vizier (Gerankhar), a wise and merciful man, on the other. The king gave his seal to the vizier and built the city of Gondishapur on saline grounds as a gift for his son. Until he grew up, Shapur did not get away from Ardashir for a moment. One day, Ardashir told his wise vizier, "You need to send someone to the enlightened king of India, Kaede, to ask my question." He prepared gifts and sent them to India with a messenger. The vizier went before the king and asked, "Ardashir wants to know when he will find respite from war and bring peace and calm to the world?" Kaede gazed at the stars and said, "When Ardashir's bloodline is mixed with Mihrak Nushzad's blood (The ruler of Jahrom during the reign of Ardashir I. When Ardashir went to war, he took the opportunity to plunder his crown and treasury. Ardashir fought and killed him.), there will be peace in the nation, and you will achieve what you wish." He then gave the messenger gifts and sent him off. Ardashir was distressed and said, "I will never see that day. For I only have a daughter from Mihrak seen by no one, whom it is said resides in Jahrom." He immediately sent cavalry to Jahrom. When the girl found out that they were after her, she immediately went to a village and hid.

Some time passed. One day, the king and Shapur went out on a hunt. The cavalry dispersed. Shapur found himself in a vast wilderness with trees and fruits, and headed toward the village.

There, he saw a beautiful girl busy pulling water from a well. The girl came to Shapur and praised him. "Do not trouble yourself, alluring girl. My servants shall draw water for you." He then called them near the well, but they couldn›t pull the bucket up. When Shapur realized that they were incapable of doing so, he went himself and pulled the bucket. The bucket was extremely heavy. Shapur knew that the girl was a descendant of heroes to have such strength.

After Shapur pulled the bucket of water, the girl said, "The Lord protect you, Shapur, son of Ardashir!" "How did you recognize me?" inquired Shapur. "I've heard plenty about your heroism," said the girl, "You look like Bahman." "Of what descent are you?" asked Shapur. "I am the daughter of a farmer," said the girl. Shapur knew that she was lying, and guaranteed her safety. "I am the daughter of Mihrak Nushzad," revealed the girl, "I came to this village in fear of the king, and draw water from wells for a living." Shapur invited her to be godly, and married her in secrecy. Nine months later, the girl gave birth to a boy like Esfandiar. Shapur named him Ohrmazd. The king was hidden from the public for seven years. Then, one day, Ardashir took Shapur on a seven-day hunt.

Ohrmazd left the house in secret and played polo with his friends. The king reached the playground. A child threw the ball at the king, and none of the boys could dare return it. Ohrmazd came running and returned the ball to them. The knew anything. The king ordered to have him brought before himself, and asked the child, who said without hesitation, "I am the son of Shapur, and your grandson. My mother is the daughter of Mihrak." They called Shapur, and he reaffirmed the child's claim. The king became happy. Upon seeing the joy in his father, Shapur told him the whole story. The king ordered to make a golden throne, and poured gold and coins over the boy. He then plucked him out of the coins, put a golden crown on his head, seated him on the throne, and gave money to the destitute. He held a ceremony and told the elders, "The Indian king said that on the day that my descendants mix with Mihrak's; fate will turn in our favor. This is the eighth year, and I am elated."

During his rule, Ardashir accomplished great things that made his name eternal. He established kindness and justice in all the countries subjected to his rule, and tended to his army diligently. He taught their children horse-riding and warfare, and trained those interested in arts. His army grew in number, and people came to join Ardashir's army from every location. He hired specialists in his court and barred the illiterate. He valued writers and administrators, and ordered Shapur, "Do not bring suffering to the people for treasure. Always seek knowledge and wisdom, and keep away from greed. Give to the poor, build the country, and give specialists appropriate jobs. Recognize and value the knowledgeable, and keep the unintelligent away from yourself. Replace the old with the wise and learned youth." He trained his army not to harm people or plunder the cities they ventured into, and to always keep God in mind. During his reign, there was no one in need. People who suffered unfairly would go to the city square at dawn, and a just judge chosen by Ardashir would instate justice. He established justice and altruism around the world, exempted drought-stricken lands from taxes, and gave seeds, tools of farming, and cows to farmers.

During his time, people were harmless, and nobody bothered anyone. He ruled Rome, India, China, and Turkey, and they obeyed him. He would always remind heads of state that only a good name remains; and advised Ohrmazd against raising people's taxes. "I take one-tenth from the wealthy and spend it on my army," he said, "You should do the same. Always be generous and help the oppressed. Never become arrogant; spread the seeds of nobility wherever you are."

One day, an old man named Kharad went before Ardashir and said, "Your justice has spread to the point where even the animals come to you. Good for us to live under your rule and be graced by your visage. You kept the nation safe from war, bloodshed, and plunder. You gave prominence to wisdom and knowledge, spread justice, and made the nation God-worshippers."

Ardashir lived on until the age of seventy-eight when he fell ill. He gave Shapur many advices, and asked him to live by his law, "Cruelty will be the end of monarchy Avoid greed, and spend the nation's treasure on the people. Make the eyes of the guilty long for rest, and give to the helpless as much as possible. Do not procrastinate, and do not give positions to fools. Always heed the best words. Continue along my path, and do not torment the nation. I ask the Lord to keep you safe from evil. I turned six towns to cities during my forty years and two months. The cities of Ardashir-Khwarrah in Khuzestan, Gondishapur, Maysan, the Euphrates, Berkeyeh Ardashir and Rame Ardashir in Fars, and Ohrmazd." He then closed his eyes, and was put in a casket, then buried in a tomb.

ushirvan sat upon the throne and advised the elders, "I ask you to remember God at all times, for the good and bad in us comes from Him. They should help the poor and make them needless. Do not pollute your tongues with lies. Any Iranian who comes before our court will benefit from our treasury. He divided the nation into four regions. The first was Khorasan; the second was Qom and Isfahan, the third spanned Armenia to Ardabil, and the fourth encompassed Pars and Ahvaz all the way to the shores of the Caspian Sea. He then sent people all around to rebuild ruins and help the poor, and raised the taxes on the wealthy by a factor of ten. All kings came to him to pay royalties. He did nothing but good, and entrusted the administration of government and army to Babak, the wise mobad, assembled a huge army from across Iran, and decreed, "Make sure no one sleeps at night having suffered from the army." The entire army congratulated him and screamed in unison, "We have learned since King Fereydoun not to do evil or any wrongdoing to the people." Hearing these words made tears stream from his eyes.

He ordered to build a wall along the border of Iran to prevent enemies from attacking and plundering Iranian villages and farmers. Then, a giant iron gate was built, and guards were placed atop walls. Thereafter, the king went to the sea and reached Alani. There, he saw a land in ruin, and sent a representative to the Alans and asked them not to attack Iran and abide by Iranian rule. They gathered around, came to the king with plenty of gifts and taxes, and bowed before him and made a pact. The king forbore their past transgressions, and ordered to build up their nation and shield it against enemies with a wall. Then, he went to India. All the elders came to him with an abundance of royalties and gifts. A messenger informed him of the plunder of Guilan. On his way, the king reached Baluchistan, and men and women put down their swords and surrendered. By Anushirvan's decree, the land was made so secure that shepherds would leave their herds on mountains and hills. The king went to Guilan, killed many soldiers, and imprisoned the captives. The women and children came to him, and expressed regret about their unsavory deeds. The king gave them amnesty.

Anushirvan took his military toward Madain. On his journey, Mondher the Arab met him, and the king was delighted. "Are you not the king of the world?" posed Mondher, "Then why has the Caesar of Rome appointed himself our king, and asked us to obey him? What is your command?" Anushirvan fumed, sent a messenger to Caesar, and asked him to stop his mischievous deeds and leave Arabs in peace; for they were a protectorate of Iran and took orders from Anushirvan." Caesar replied harshly to the messenger. Anushirvan was enraged; and sent Mondher to Rome along with 30,000 swordsmen. Earlier, he wrote a letter to Caesar and asked him to stop bothering Arabs so that Iran's king would permit him to remain on

Rome's throne. The messenger delivered the letter to Caesar, who replied angrily, "A Roman will never pay taxes to an Iranian. We will no longer pay you royalties, for we are not afraid of your elephants and soldiers. Now it is time for you to pay us royalties."

The messenger brought the letter to the king, and he consulted with the elders for three days and moved his army to Rome on the fourth. When he reached Azerbaijan, he went to Azargoshasp's tomb and prayed. Then, he ventured forth to Rome. Kings came to him from all around to show their servitude. When approaching Rome, the king warned his army, "If one person disobeys me, or does something without my information, harms the rich or the poor, tramples farms, or picks a fruit without the gardener's permission, I will slice them in half, as the Lord is my witness." The soldiers in every tent were notified of Anushirvan's remarks, "We will spill your blood if you treat people unjustly and harshly." According to Anushirvan's justice, before his conquests, he would send an honest messenger to the king to address the problem without war and blood-spilling. He would fight and bring justice by the sword if they didn't surrender.

Along the way, they reached Shurab, witnessed a towering fortress, and attacked it from four sides with catapults. In the end, the fortress of the Catholicos fell. The king loaded elephants with its treasure and sent them to Iran. On their way back, they reached another fort called Arayesh which housed Caesar's wealth. The soldiers unleashed a rain of arrows upon the fort, and its people surrendered. The king took hold of Caesar's entire treasury, and sent it back to Iran. The afflicted people came to the king, and asked him to guarantee their safety. The king ended the war, bestowed gold and coins upon the people, and headed to Rome.

Caesar sent an army commanded by Porphyry to stop the Iranians. The Persian army killed an abundance of Roman soldiers, and Porphyry fled. The Iranians gave chase, and reached Fort Qalynyws. Initially, there was resistance, but they finally surrendered to the Iranian army. The king mounted their wealth on camels, and headed toward Antakya. He waited outside the city for three days, hoping that they would surrender. On the fourth day, they attacked the city. The Roman army dispersed, and the fort›s elders gave their wealth to Anushirvan. The king sent them all to Madain. The city of Antakya was built on water, and Anushirvan was pleased with it. He ordered to build a city like Antakya in Iran, named Zibkhosrow. The king appointed a righteous Christian man as the king of the city.

Porphyry went to Caesar and informed him about the war. The Caesar gathered around the elders, and realized that he was powerless to confront the Iranian army. He sent sixty wise mobads, supervised by Mehras, to Anushirvan with precious gifts, and distanced himself from his previous statements. The king was happy about the wise man's words, forgave their sins, and headed to Rome. Anushirvan entrusted the rule to Shiruy Bahram, and moved his army to Jordan. The world lived in dread and hope of Anushirvan. He held a sword on one hand, and dispensed kindness and affection with the other.

## Bozorgmehr

One night, Anushirvan dreamed that a beautiful tree had grown next to the throne, and saw a sabretooth boar sitting next to it. He woke up downhearted. Many scientists and dream interpreters were brought to the court, but none could make sense of it.

So he sent messengers all around to bring him experts. One of the elders named "Azadsarv" headed toward Marv. There, there was a scientist who taught children about Zand and Avesta. His best student was Bozorgmehr.

When the king›s messenger saw his knowledge and steadfast belief, he stopped and inquired about the king›s order. The master responded, "This is not my profession, and I do not know dream interpretation." Bozorgmehr overheard them and told the master, "I can do this. I know dream interpretation." The king›s messenger insisted that the master permit Bozorgmehr to interpret the dream. The master sent him back with the messenger downhearted. "I will only tell the king," said Bozorgmehr. Then, they gave him a horse, coins, and suitable attire, and took him to the palace. They reached a lush green place and rested for some time. Bozorgmehr slept under a tree›s shade, and pulled a curtain on his face. A black serpent crept up on him, went up his face, and headed to the tree. When Bozorgmehr opened his eyes; the serpent escaped and disappeared. The king›s messenger was shocked, and pondered, "This child will become a powerful man."

They came to the palace, and the messenger recounted to the king the whole story. Bozorgmehr told the king, "In your harem, a young man has disguised himself as a woman. Bring them here and let's find him." The king gave the order, but they couldn›t find the man. "They should remove their clothes," said Bozorgmehr. The women did as he asked, and they saw a handsome young man among the maids, the brother of the Khan of Chach's daughter. The girl was questioned. "He is my younger brother," she said, "and I did this to protect him."

By the king›s order, they were both killed. The king gave Bozorgmehr gold and coins, and kept him in his palace. He continued to learn knowledge and wisdom from great masters until he became superior to all of his contemporary scientists. One day during a celebration, the king gathered his scientists and asked them to entertain him with a wise remark. Each of the intellectuals stood up and said something. Bozorgmehr stood up, asked for permission, and said, "I envy those who can say their intention briefly. The fool and the unwise speak at length and fall short in understanding. Do not speak extensively so you are not humbled before the people." Likewise, he would speak in short and meaningful sentences. The elders and the king were in awe. The king ordered him to have his name written as the greatest intellectual of the period. Whenever he had the chance, the kind would seek solitude with him and hear his magnificent remarks. He would always pose his questions to Bozorgmehr, who would always answer the king fittingly.

# Yazdgerd

In the month of Esfand, Yazdgerd took the throne. He ruled for sixteen years, and sought a good name. During his reign, the people were in peace. At this time, Omar was the caliph of Arabs and sent Sa'd Waqqas to fight Iran. Upon hearing the news of the Arab invasion, he appointed Rostam, Son of Hormoz, a wise and cunning hero, the commander of his army. Rostam knew astronomy. He gathered around heroes and fought the Arabs for thirty months.

Many were killed on both sides. One day, he took his astrolabe, gazed upon the stars, and beat his head in angst. What he had seen, he wrote to his brother in sorrow, "The Sassanid Kingdom will be destroyed, and Iranians will shed tears for their king's demise. We will be defeated in this war, and they will rule us for four-hundred years. Gather what you have and go to Azerbaijan with our mother. Relay my words to her and pay my respects. I will not survive this war. After me, do not spare any efforts in assisting the king. Always fear God and give to other, for the world will endure for none." He sealed the letter, and sent it to his brother.

He sent a messenger to Sa'd, and asked, "Who is your king? Why have you invaded Iran, and what do you aim to achieve? If you want to live in Iran, I will suggest to the king to give you wealth. But know that taking over Iran is impossible for you. Send a messenger to tell me what you want." Sa'd welcomed

Rostam›s messenger and read the letter. Then, he wrote his response in Arabic. He spoke of the Prophet Muhammad (SAW), Tawhid (monotheism), and the Quran. He wrote of paradise, hell, and the afterlife, "If your king accepts our faith, we will stop war and give him the throne. However, if he doesn›t; our only choice is war and bloodshed." The messenger returned to Rostam with patched clothes. They prepared a majestic seat for him, but he sat on the ground, and gave him the letter without paying his respects. After reading the letter, Rostam fumed and said, "Death is a preferable alternative to bringing joy to the enemy."

The two armies faced each other, and the drumbeats of war started. The fighting continued for three days. Rostam's lips were parched from thirst. At last, Rostam and Sa'd fought each other away from their armies. Rostam struck Sa'd's horse with his sword, and the animal collapsed and so did he. Rostam raised his sword to separate his head. An Arab soldier struck his hip from behind, Sa'd stood up, incised Rostam›s head with a blade, and tore up his neck and body thereafter. Rostam fell down and died. After seeing their commander dead, the Iranian army fled. Many of them were slain, and the rest came to Yazdgerd in Baghdad. Farrokhzad (Iranian hero) attacked Arab lancers in Arvandrud and Karkheh and killed many; but the Iranian army still suffered defeat.

He returned to the king and asked him to go to Narun forest to gather an army from Amol and Sari to counter the Arabs.

On the next day, Yazdgerd took the throne and consulted with the elders, but they opposed his plan. "I believe we should fight to our last breaths," said the king. The elders praised him. Then, they ventured to Khorasan to seek help from the Chinese emperor and the Turks. They decided to send a messenger to Mahoe Suri, the frontier general of Marv with many soldiers, to bring help; for he was trained and given power by the king. Farrokhzad was familiar with Mahoe's mischievous nature, and tried to persuade the king against it. Yazdgerd, however, wanted to give it a try.

Then, the elders and the king started. The king asked Chinese merchants to return to their country, who obliged him with weeping and sorrowful eyes. The king went through Rey to Gorgan accompanied by the army. Then, he wrote a letter to Mahoe, and announced their defeat and Rostam's death and said, "The Arabs have advanced up to Ctesiphon. Come to our help with your army." Then, he wrote a letter to Tous, appreciated his help, promised him greater gifts, recounted the Arab invasion of Iran, and said, "Anushirvan had seen this war in his dream, and it has come true." He explained, "We are in Khorasan, and Farrokhzad is fighting the enemy with his army." He asked him to come to his help with an army and write a letter to the elders of all cities to send food, horses, and their wealth to the king to allow him to resist the Arabs. He and the army moved to Nishapur, and thence to Tous. Mahoe greeted him. Farrokhzad was elated, and entrusted the kingdom to him and went to Rey to fight the Arabs.

After some time, Mahoe contemplated becoming the king. At that time, a hero named Bijan was the ruler of Samarqand. Mahoe wrote him a letter, asked for his presence, and promised to make him king of Iran. Bijan consulted with the elders, and decided to dispatch an army to fight Yazdgerd and take the throne. Bijan›s Turkish army came from Bokhara to Marv. Mahoe told the King of Iran that the Turks had stabbed them in the back and came for war. Yazdgerd and his army went to fight the Turks. The king killed many of them; and the Iranian army turned their backs against the king. He found out about Mahoe›s trickery. The king was left alone, and desperately went inside a well to hide. The soldiers did not find him and returned. The miller, Khosrow, entered and saw a hero with beautiful attire and a king›s crown, sitting on a stone. The king told him that he was the commander of the Persian army, and had fled Turan.

The miller brought him some bread and curd. The king hid in the mill for three days. Mahoe sent his people around, and found the king at last. He called the miller, who said that he had given the man shelter out of fear. Mahoe asked him to behead the king at once. A mobad named Radoy told Mahoe, "O ignoble man! Have you ever seen a land with two kings? Let go of this villainous thought, for people will utter your name in disgrace for posterity." The elders all opposed him, and complained about the king's death. They wanted to gather the Iranian army, and go to the king to apologize and fight the Arabs with him shoulder to shoulder.

The mobad's counseling was a difficult pill for treacherous Mahoe to swallow. Mahoe's secret was revealed, so he called his son to consult him. "If the king is killed by your hand," he said, "All of Iran will rise against you and an army from China will seek to destroy you." Then, Mahoe went toward the mill with a cavalry. It was the middle of the month of Khordad, and he asked the king to take the king's clothes and kill him. The miller entered, took the king's clothes, and approached him as if to whisper something, and plunged a dagger into the king's stomach. Yazdgerd collapsed to the ground; and his blood trickled on the bread and curd before him. He was slain innocently and by someone he had nurtured. The cavalry brought the king's items to Mahoe and threw his corpse into the water.

At dawn, the people standing around the water saw the king's body. Several monks and people dragged Yazdgerd's body out of the water and mourned for him. Then, they build a tomb in a garden, purified his body with musk and camphor, and buried him. Then, they informed Mahoe Suri, who ordered to kill the monks who mourned for Yazdgerd and buried him. Then, he called his supporters and told them that he intended to become the king. They told him that the king's ring had the name of Yazdgerd engraved, and all of Iran were his supporters. "The people and the army will not obey you," they said. One of them suggested, "Gather the elders and tell everyone that Yazdgerd, who raised me, entrusted the crown to me and made me his successor before his death. He asked me not to leave the king's crown to the enemy."

Mahoe did so, assumed the throne, and ruled Khorasan. He gave Balkh and Herat to his son, gave positions to rascals, and overthrew the intellectuals. He then assembled a massive army and went to Bokhara, Samarqand, and Chach to kill Bijan. Bijan heard the news about Mahoe's succession and that he sought war, and asked, "Who gave him the throne?!" "It was arranged for Mahoe to send you Yazdgerd's throne to Chach, but he has changed his mind and taken the throne."

Bijan assembled his army and came to Bokhara. Upon seeing his army, Mahoe almost died in terror. A war commenced between them. Barsam raised Mahoe by the belt in the middle of the river and pounded him to the dirt from the saddle. He then took him to Bijan with his hands tied. "O wretched devil, why did you kill that just and powerful king?" He ordered to have Mahoe›s hands, legs, ears, and nose cut off, and put him on the river›s hot stones. He fell unconscious from horror and agony. They burned Mahoe›s three sons along with him so that they would not have any descendants. The Arabs dominated large swaths of Iran, and ruled for four-hundred years.

THE END